The Boy Who Invented Himself

By Pierre V Comtois

"The Boy Who Invented Himself," by Pierre V. Comtois. ISBN 978-1-63868-217-2 (softcover). Cover image respective copyright holders.

Published 2025 by Virtualbookworm.com Publishing Inc., P.O. Box 9949, College Station, TX 77842, US. ©2025, Pierre V. Comtois. All rights reserved. No part of this publication may be reproduced, stored in a retrieval system, or transmitted in any form or by any means, electronic, mechanical, recording or otherwise, without the prior written permission of Pierre V. Comtois.

Some years ago, in the old mill town of Lowell, Massachusetts, lived a boy named Guy DeMonde who was at once a dreamer and sometimes a loner. When he wasn't off by himself dreaming in his tree house, Guy spent time with a tight knit group of neighborhood pals with whom he embarked on the usual round of small adventures that built camaraderie and fond memories. Then, one day, he and his friends encountered the greatest challenge of their young lives: a new kid in the neighborhood whose lifestyle contradicted many of the beliefs they had always taken for granted. Now, Guy in particular, must find a way to avoid the path of least resistance, learn to tell good from bad, and finally re-invent himself with his own personality, one that didn't rely on others to fashion and that would preserve and strengthen his values to withstand the test of time. Will he succeed? It's a question that demands Guy's story to be read, cherished, and thought about long after the final page has been turned.

CONTENTS

FOREWORD

I really never considered writing a book like this. What I prefer to write is science fiction or fantasy, but Noel kept urging me (in a nice way!) to write about something closer to home. She suggested that I write what I know about like Lucy Maude Montgomery or Earl Hamner or even Mark Twain! "Imagine if you wrote the Tom Sawyer of the 1960s?" she said. Yeah, right! But that was typical of Noel Archambault who moved in across the street from me when we were kids on Desrosiers Street. Boy, do I remember those days when we were always at loggerheads, usually arguing about books. She preferred the classics of western literature and I science fiction and fantasy. Which is where the Mark Twain stuff came in. She's never completely given up trying to get me to "broaden my horizons" as she puts it. Still, we've long since arrived at an entente (a popular word back in the sixties when we were growing up) All that said, her suggestion about writing something down to earth was more likely prompted by the success of her own book that she titled *Sometimes a Warm Rain Falls.* (I have to admit liking that title; it has a very Ray Bradbury-ish ring to it) In it, she wrote about her experiences after moving from New York to Lowell. More specifically, her move into our old neighborhood on Desrosiers Street and the new life she found there with the other kids on the block (including me) She took a lot of pleasure writing and revisiting those years and was mildly surprised at the success of the book. It convinced her that there were plenty of people beside herself, who were interested in reading about her experiences (although somewhat fictionalized to protect the innocent!) As a result, she thought it would be interesting to have the story told from another point of view, perhaps recounting events from the years before she moved to Lowell. But I have a sneaking suspicion that she had the idea all along. Why else would she at one point, have suggested that I keep a diary the way she did when she first moved to Desrosiers Street? She'd used entries from the diary (properly sanitized to be sure) as chapter headings in *Sometimes A Warm Rain Falls* and thought I might use the same gimmick for my prequel. But as I told her then, "Diaries are for girls, boys keep journals." Well, I never did keep that journal, at least back in the day, but later, I did put some thoughts down on paper for no other reason than for self reflection purposes. In rereading them, I found that they could be useful in putting book together. But instead of using them for chapter headings, I decided to use excerpts from the science fiction novel I was writing at the time because some parts of it did relate somehow to the action that takes place in the main story. The reader will have to decide if they work the way I intended. The only other thing readers ought to know I guess, is that most of the action in the book will take place over a few years in my life, from the summer of 1964 to the spring of 1967 with some flashback information to fill in the back story when needed.

Guy DeMonde
20--

Dedicated to the family's third generation (so far!):
Ellie, Suzy, Lucas, Allie, Jacob, Eli, Karelia, and
Sophia. May their childhoods be happy ones with no
mistakes in them.

INTRODUCTION

I suppose the first thing I ought to do before deep diving in to the story is to set the scene. That's what novelists are supposed to do, so here goes:

The first thing you noticed was the quiet.

That's a funny sounding line to begin in setting the scene, I know, but it's important in describing what it was like in my neighborhood in those still sleepy days of the mid 1960s when there was no such thing as computers, the internet, or cell phones and most families had only a single car (or sometimes none); and when fathers took that one car to work, well, everyone else was grounded. So, during work days and school days, roads were mostly deserted, and quiet reigned so that you could hear the trees rustling in even the slightest breeze and solitary birds calling from far beyond the farthest tree you could see. In fact, the only sounds that might break the silence was the faraway drone of a distant plane or heat bugs (cicadas) on hot summer afternoons.

Sometimes the quiet might also be broken with the arrival of the milkman or the breadman, both long since vanished from city streets. The milkman, of course, arrived in the morning, filling milk boxes on people's front steps every other day with quarts of fresh milk from local farms and dairies. Breadmen used to pull up in front of homes and, pulling down the tail gate of a station wagon, maybe, would display everything from loaves of Wonder Bread to twinkies for discerning housewives. But when they left, quiet would once again settle over the neighborhood. It would stay that way until mid-afternoon when school let out. Then, after changing into their play clothes, kids would storm the streets and play hide and seek, red light, or simon says with their laughter and shouting filling the air clean to supper time. Night came too early in the winter for after supper play and most kids retreated into the warm indoors to concentrate on homework, but in summers, when the days were longer, out they'd come again and in my neighborhood, that meant mostly waiting till dusk when kick the can would be played in the gathering gloom with the only dread being when the streetlights might came on signaling the end of the fun. At home again, it was time for homework and washing up. On Saturdays, the routine was altered to include baths (showers weren't to become a thing for a few more years yet) and in pajamas and nightgowns, kids would gather 'round the TV set to watch *Lost in Space* or *My Three Sons*, or *The Patty Duke Show*.

Anyway, that's the way most days passed in a time that I used to call "the golden age" when kids were oblivious to whatever might be happening in the larger world and each day passed one into another with barely a care at all. And on Desrosiers Street in particular, it seemed there couldn't be a better place to live than in that neighborhood. In those days of the early to mid-1960s it seemed to be perfection where everything was in equilibrium: just the right time and place with the best friends, solid family values, and loving parents. It was also perfectly situated just on the border of the city on one hand where me and my friends could ride our bikes into town to go to the movies and the country on the other where our bikes could also reach open woods and farmland in a matter of minutes. Or at least that's the way it all seemed at time. In reality, it might not have been as perfect as all that (there were punk kids to worry about and tests to take at school and even the odd dentist's appointment), but it wasn't nearly as unreal as people began to claim years later. In short, the Desorisers Street neighborhood was as good a place to grow up as any kid could want.

However, the city of Lowell itself, where our neighborhood was partly located, might have left something to be desired. The city was still much the way writer and former citizen, Jack Kerouac, left it years before when he abandoned the old mill town in the 1950s. Located in the long valley where the sluggish Merrimack River flowed, Lowell continued to sleep drowsily in the heat of summer and the cold of winter. Its silent red brick mills that lined the river and miles of canals stood nearly empty. Over the decades, most of the jobs they used to offer had fled and those that remained provided residents mainly with a middle to lower middle class living. For that reason, most people who worked in Lowell, lived in the double and triple decker tenements that crowded inner city neighborhoods. Lowell itself was a small city as cities went. It used to be bigger, but over the years parts of it were lopped off to form such adjoining towns as Chelmsford and Tewksbury and Dracut which were given over largely to farmland.

Meanwhile, back on Desrosiers Street, that border land between city and country, there was plenty to hold the imagination of kids and in particular, there was the Jorgenson's yard. The home of my best friend Jiff Jorgenson, it presented a wonderland of physical features that fed into our imaginations. Much as the early explorers of North America wondered at the diversity of landscape the continent offered in plains and mountains, desert and lake, forest and swamp so too did the Jorgenson's back yard seem to us. In our imaginations, it seemed to be a strange and unexplored continent filled with a diversity of locales suited to any boy's spirit of adventure: There was Buck Rogers' spaceship (the Jorgenson's front porch), there the surface of an alien world (a front yard filled with bushes and hedges and an adjoining open field), here streams of hot flowing lava (a wooded brook that flowed deep down beyond the back yard where downed trees afforded precarious bridges over the water), or menacing quicksand (estuaries of the brook filled with frogs and tadpoles), a Nazi prison camp (the Jorgenson's garage with a trap door for escaping POWs), or a pirate's secret hideout (an abandoned tree house down in the swamp).

All together, Lowell and Dracut, Desrosiers Street and the Jorgenson's, town and country, formed a world and a time that in many ways should have vanished long before, but somehow managed to hang on a while longer as if waiting to work their magic on one last subject, one last boy, lucky enough to live there, namely me!

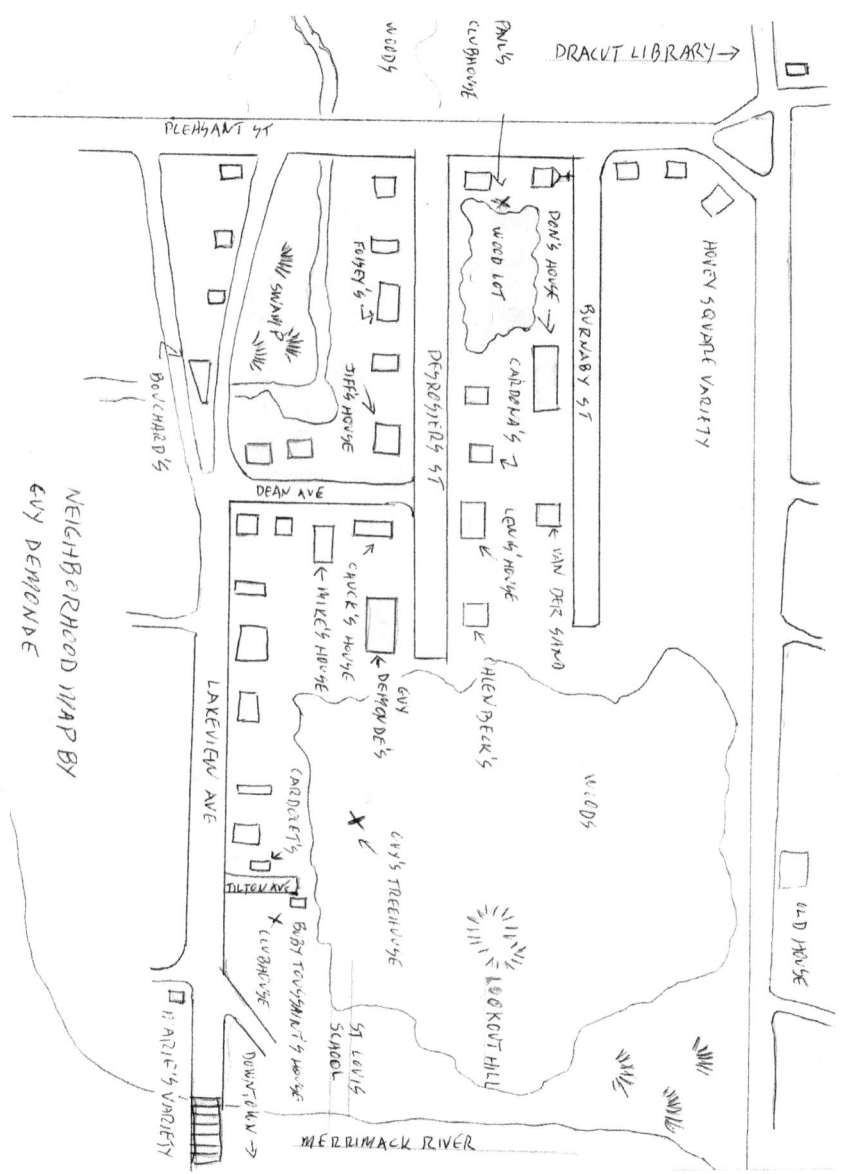

xiii

CHAPTER ONE

How Guy met Jiff

Nick Tropoli stood outside the gates of the Inter Planet Space Force training academy, bag in hand.

Being named a cadet was the answer to a long standing dream and he looked forward to the lessons and the drills and to graduating a second lieutenant in the Inter Planet Space Force and to some day commanding his own ship.

More immediately, he looked forward to making new friends among his fellow cadets. Who knew? Maybe within these gates was someone who would become a lifelong friend. Someone with whom he would share countless adventures and hair raising dangers as they enforced the law in the solar system!

Eagerly, he stepped inside the gates and was quickly assaulted by the barking voice of an upper classman who ordered him into ranks with other cadets.

Nick added himself to the long line, right next to a lanky, blond young man standing at stiff attention, chin tucked inside the collar of his uniform.

"They don't waste any time here, do they?" grumbled Nick.

"You're telling me," replied the other.

"What's your name? Mine's Nick, Nick Tropoli."

1

"Dan Montez," said the other young man, not daring to turn his head.

Gateway to the Future
Guy DeMonde

If a story has to start some place, then why not here?

Why not in the swamp behind the Jorgenson's house?

There, two young boys carefully balanced themselves as they inched along the wooden frame of a discarded screen door the better to reach the part of the swamp where the water was deeper.

"Careful," said the one with the crew cut and patched up navy blue pants. "Don't want to fall into all this mucky water."

"And scare the pollywogs away," said the other, holding out his arms to help keep his balance as he reached the farthest edge of the screen door.

Hoppy toads had been plentiful behind the Rocheleau's garage the year before and Guy DeMonde and Jiff Jorgenson had reaped a rich harvest of them for occupation in the paradise they'd fashioned for them in an old wheel barrel. But despite piling in plenty of soil, leaving a little swimming hole in the center, and transplanting grasses and ferns from the swamp, the small toads they'd collected refused to remain in the wheel barrel. (They'd even provided them with a plentiful supply of ants and spiders taken from among the interstices of the stone wall that encircled part of the Jorgenson's back yard) The failure to hold their charges in no way dimmed the boys' enthusiasm for the project so that this year, they were determined to make a success of it.

"Where'd we get the name hoppy toads for the baby frogs we caught last year anyway?" asked Guy.

"My mother," replied Jiff, the slightly taller of the two. "And if the pollywogs are out, the hoppy toads won't be far behind."

"I think that chicken wire fencing we found will be just the thing to hold the toads in the wheel barrel this time," noted Guy as he prepared to crouch down closer to the water.

"Hope so. But it's too early for them right now."

For the past couple of years the boys had found that the baby toads were most numerous behind the Rocheleau's garage where the land sloped steeply down to the moist soil that bordered the swamp. It stood to reason that the same phenomenon would occur again this spring.

Luckily for them, the Rocheleau's treated the swampy area behind their garage as if it were part of their property and dumped all manner of construction material there that the boys often used to build wharves and bridges out over the water the better to hunt frogs, look for the odd fish able to survive in the brackish waters, and of course, tadpoles that they referred to as pollywogs.

"There sure is a lot of algae floating on the water," said Guy, staring at the mass of tiny green leafage that covered virtually the whole surface of the swamp. To spot any tadpoles, they'd have to shove it aside.

"Should mean plenty of pollywogs," replied Jiff, fingering the empty peanut butter jar in his hands. "It's what they like to eat."

"Hard to believe they grow into frogs," remarked Guy.

"Yeah, and usually there's millions of 'em," replied Jiff. "So how come there end up being so few hoppy toads?"

"Dunno," said Guy, shrugging.

Algae usually meant tadpoles, or so the boys had always surmised. If asked, they wouldn't be able to say where they got the notion, just as their certain knowledge of other things had been acquired from who knew where. Notions such as the fear of dragonflies that they called "sewing needles" and because of that always kept their mouths open when one was spotted in order to keep it from sewing their lips shut. Or avoiding bats who liked nothing better than entangling their tiny feet in a person's hair. With his whiffle, Guy was relieved that he had little to fear on that account but Jiff's longer blond hair was a definite hazard.

With his own jar in hand, Guy crouched down on the edge of the screen and through a little clearing in the algae cover, he could see clouds of tadpoles swarming in the shallow water.

"Wow! There must be millions of the 'em down there!"

"Let me see," said Jiff, carefully turning around on the ball of one foot to make his way back to Guy.

The boys had been friends, best friends, for years by this time and fancied they knew each other's thoughts and movements better than anyone else. And maybe they did. At least Guy believed it. Ever since that first day they met when Guy's house on Desrosiers Street was in the final days of construction. Guy had been fooling around in a pile of sand on the property when he noticed another boy in the street looking over the new house. He waved when he saw Guy who was emboldened to go out to the street and meet the stranger.

"Hi," he'd said.

"Hi," replied Guy.

"You going to live here?" asked the stranger.

Guy nodded. "Where do you live?"

The stranger turned and pointed farther up the street to a big, two story farmhouse on the corner of Desrosiers and Dean Avenue. "Over there."

They exchanged names and Guy forgot what the rest of their conversation had been. All he remembered was that since then, they'd been inseperable. Between adventures around the neighborhood, they took turns spending time at each other's homes which offered different attractions. At Guy's, there were also his younger twin sisters, Marie and Trece, and at Jiff's, his older sister and brother, Patsy and Brent. The latter two were always teasing Jiff, calling him "Itch" with Brent giving him Indian sunburns and noogies by rubbing his knuckles vigorously on Jiff's scalp whenever he could catch him. Luckily, he seemed to ignore Guy.

And though Guy's home was new, Jiff's had been an old farmhouse complete with a big chicken coop in the deep backyard where the swamp lapped in the lower reaches. The coop was in ruins but offered amusement for the boys when they tried to cross the tangle of timbers and planking without falling in. An old outbuilding served as a garage that Mr. Jorgenson used mostly to store used bakery equipment that he planned to use when he was ready to open his own business some day. Later, the garage would be improved with an extension out the back built so that the Jorgenson's new car could fit inside. But what mattered to Jiff and Guy and their friends, was that the extension had a removable panel that could be used as a secret escape route when they played *The Great Escape* after seeing the movie on TV. There were a couple big apple trees good for climbing, pine trees and a giant maple tree in the back yard and a big open field perfect for war games and playing football with the big kids.

And then there was the swamp, of course. Actually it was part of a small stream that came from somewhere in Dracut and flowed out to Beaver Brook which emptied into the Merrimack River. But where it came past the Jorgenson's, it formed an elbow where the water grew still and stagnant and became a natural breeding ground for frogs and their associated tadpoles. An irresistable attraction for boys like Guy and Jiff and to their parents' bane.

More than once, well, all the time actually, Guy had been warned by his mother to stay away from the brook. He was never sure what her concern about it was. Was it the bugs (his mother had a fear of bees) or was it catching some disease like beri beri or malaria like the people in Tarzan movies who found themselves lost in the jungle? Or was she just afraid that he'd drown? Staring at the water in front of him with the bottom clearly visible only a few inches down, Guy scoffed at the idea of drowning in the brook. Anyway, not without some feelings of guilt, Guy routinely ignored his mother's admonitions and went to the brook all the time. Besides looking for tadpoles and frogs, he and Jiff liked to try and follow its course by walking along and jumping from one log and fallen tree branch to another without falling in the water that they pretended was boiling lava. Or finding glass bottles, tossing them into the brook on one side of Pleasant Street and then running across to the other side and trying to shatter them with rocks as they drifted from beneath the street. In winter, sometimes there was enough open water to skate on when it froze. Anyway, when all was said and done, Guy had no doubt that his mother's fears were unfounded. Nothing had ever happened to him as a result of fooling around in the brook.

The irony was that when he and Jiff did have misadventures, they tended to happen elsewhere than the brook. Like the time they walked up through the field across the street from the Jorgenson's in order to reach an abandoned shed on the other side. They had no problem walking through the waist high grass and when they reached the shed, they found it locked and a mysterious metal plate on the ground beneath an old grape arbor. Unable to lift the plate they'd guessed it might be covering the entrance to Hell! And maybe it did because they hadn't left that field yet when they began to itch and scratch. And by the time they reached the street, it felt like they were being stung all over!

Luckily, Mrs. Jorgenson had been sitting in the front yard hanging the laundry when the boys rushed up to her almost in tears. Quickly, she figured out what was wrong and had them strip to their underwear and when they did, turned the garden hose on them. They'd been covered with angry red ants whose tiny stings had become unendurable!

Guy and Jiff had shared plenty of other adventures since that first historic meeting in front of Guy's house including nearly falling from an old tree house down in the swamp built by the Rochleau boys, sinking into piles of rain soaked sand that acted like quicksand when they'd gone to explore the foundations of a new apartment complex being built down the street (they'd lost their shoes deep in the wet sand that time), and found themselves locked in the Jorgenson's garage all afternoon when Jiff's parents had gone for a drive.

Another time, Guy had gone down to the bottom of Desrosiers Street to meet Jiff as he was dropped off by the school bus. Coming from behind the bus and crossing the street, he'd been struck by a car. Luckily it had been coming to a stop for the bus when it hit Guy so that he just stumbled to the tarmac and did a somersault or two. But he was so panicked, he immediately got up and, not waiting to confront the driver, ran home as fast as he could. There, for some reason, he'd hid under his bed until Jiff arrived in a police car showing the way to the DeMonde home! Lucky guy!

Oh, Guy and Jiff were thick as thieves all right. That first meeting in front of Guy's house had proved an epochal event in their lives and though the two boys were different physically (where Guy had dark brown hair [when it was allowed to grow out], Jiff was blond; where Guy was of average height, Jiff was tall for his age) they were virtually identical where it counted: they were both somewhat bold and adventurous and took full advantage of the opportunities given them from living on Desrosiers Street with its fields and woods and old houses and abandoned outbuildings. And very soon, they were destined to share other interests that would deepen their friendship including discovering comic books and science fiction first in the form of movies and television programs and then in books. The combination would inspire intense new interests that for Guy would last a lifetime but for Jiff would prove merely transitory. Something that would contribute to their eventual parting of the ways many years in the future. But for now, that first meeting had initiated what Guy would later characterize as a golden age for the two of them that would last for many years.

Crouching on the edge of the old screen door, Guy bent forward, his jar poised to scoop a few dozen tadpoles...for what reason, he and Jiff hadn't really thought that far ahead. It was enough to be fascinated at seeing so many of the wriggling creatures in one place and not being able to just let them alone.

"Hey!" shouted Guy as Jiff made his way back along the screen. "I saw somethin'!"

"More pollywogs?"

"Yeah! No! I mean it was a pollywog but the biggest one I ever saw! It was huge!"

"C'mon!"

"I'm positive! It was twenty times bigger than all the others!"

"Lemme see."

"Watch out! You're too close," warned Guy as the swamp water rose around his Keds and getting his feet wet. "The screen's sinking!"

Jiff halted and attempted to back away but it was too late.

Losing his balance, Guy pitched forward into the water. With a splash, he found himself sitting waist deep in the now turgid water; strings of green algae draping his knees.

"Jiff!"

"I'm sorry! I'm sorry!" But as the water soaked up around his ankles, the last thing Jiff was thinking about was helping his friend out of the muck. Scampering along the frame of the screen door, he broke for the muddy shore.

By then, Guy had lifted himself out of the water and was right behind him. He was soaked from the waist down with mud and algea streaking the pants that had once been part of his school uniform.

"Aw, man! You look awful," said Jiff.

"My mother's gonna kill me!" Attempting to wipe away the mess covering his pants, Guy began to make his way up the slope to the Jorgenson's back yard. With every step he could feel the water in his sneakers squishing.

"You better get home and change," advised Jiff, barely able to keep from laughing despite his friend's predicament.

"Sure, but how am I gonna do it without my mother finding out? If she catches me, you won't see me again for a week."

Jiff shrugged. "Want me to get her attention her while you sneak into your room?"

Guy shook his head. "That'll never work. I'll have to try and sneak in when she goes out in the yard or something."

"Well, rotsa ruck," said Jiff, aware that he'd have his own problems explaining his wet sneakers to *his* mother.

"Thanks," said Guy, not at all comfortable with the way Jiff quickly dismissed the situation. It was careless incidents like the dunking he'd just received, that made Guy wonder about Jiff. Did he really care that it had been his fault that Guy ended up soaked?

Sometimes, like when Jiff would abandon him on hot summer days to go swimming in the Foisy's pool down the street (who were friends with the Jorgenson's), he had his doubts. But as quickly as they arose, he forgot them, the ties of friendship being too strong as yet to take them seriously.

Meanwhile, he'd been making his way across the Jorgenson's field to Dean Avenue then up to Desrosiers Street. Guy knew it would be practically impossible to get past his mother especially if his sisters spotted him first, they were sure to tattle on him. He was resigned to discovery but that wouldn't stop him from at least giving sneaking in a try.

Scouting out the house from a distance, he didn't see his mother in the yard nor his sisters. He made his way to the back door and peeked inside. It was spring and the weather was warm enough for the inside door to be left open. That was good. It reduced the chance of its squeaking giving him away. He inched his way inside, easing the storm door shut behind him. So far, so good. He'd almost made it to his room when he was stopped by a familiar voice.

"Guy DeMonde!" said his mother, but there was no pleasure in her voice.

He was doomed.

CHAPTER TWO

How Guy discovered comic books

The cadets, Nick Tropoli and Dan Montez among them, were taken on a field trip to Mars as part of their survival training. There, Nick learned how to operate in low gravity conditions and how to find his way through a blinding sandstorm.

Right along side him was his new friend Dan. They helped each other out of tight spots and learned the ropes together. They became a team.

It was during the long trip to Mars on one of the slower and more old fashioned Inter Planet transports that Nick discovered ancient adventure tapes from the twentieth century. They would become a lifelong source of entertainment and leisure for him.

"Mars is great fun," observed Dan. "But I could do without this heavy space suit."

"Me too," agreed Nick, heading for the airlock. "Meet you on the surface!"

Then he took the short leap out of the shuttle and felt his boots crunch upon the dry Martian soil.

Gateway to the Future
Guy DeMonde

It was rare for Jiff to call on Guy to come out and play but it did happen now and then.

Not only that, but it was still early on a Saturday morning with the sun barely above the treetops in the eastern sky.

"Jiff!" cried Guy, still rubbing the sleep from his eyes. "What're you doing here so early?"

"You're complaining? Heck, you're usually the one who comes calling for me at the crack of dawn."

"I do," admitted Guy, "but not you! I practically have to drag you out of bed."

"Well, Brent had to get up early to go somewhere and when that happens, he doesn't like to see me sleeping when he can't."

Guy pictured Brent dragging Jiff out of bed by his feet and throwing him to the bedroom floor. He'd done it before. Sometimes after Guy had come to call. Who could go back to sleep after a rough awakening like that?

"Besides," Jiff was saying, "Did you forget that they started to dig the hole for that new house going up behind the Cardona's yesterday? I want to check out those giant piles of dirt before they move them."

"Oh, yeah! Right!"

The boys couldn't help but hear the loud sounds of big tractors scooping out the soil in the lot behind the Cardona's. It was up hill from the Cardona's back yard so when the dirt began to be piled up, it seemed the piles were as high as Mount Everest, an irresistable challenge to Jiff and Guy.

There was some delay as Guy decided to dress as closely to Jiff as he could. Running back and forth from his room to the back door to study his friend's attire, he found a red checkered shirt that came somewhat close to Jiff's red plaid and not owning a pair of jeans, his patched up school uniform pants had to do for that. Of course, his black high top sneakers were the same brand as Jiff's.

"What about your breakfast?" asked his mother as Guy sped for the back door.

"Oh, yeah! Wait a minute, Jiff."

Guy threw a Pop Tart into the toaster and waited impatiently for it to finish.

"Hey, are there enough left for us?" asked Trece, smelling the pop tart from the girls' bedroom.

"Relax," said Guy over his shoulder. "There's some left."

The problem with a big family was that everything had to be carefully parceled out to make sure everyone had a share whether it was among the half dozen tarts in a box of pop tarts or a bag of chips. You couldn't just help yourself whenever you felt like it. In that respect at least, he envied life at Jiff's house. With only two other siblings, no one kept track of who might be eating someone else's share of cake.

Just then, his tart sprung from the toaster and Guy practically snatched it while it was still in the air.

"Yow!" He cried, as he bobbled the hot tart in his hands while heading to the door.

"About time," complained Jiff, as they left the yard.

"You should complain," said Guy, blowing on the tart to cool it enough to eat. "You keep me waiting often enough."

"Lemme have a piece," said Jiff by way of reply.

Guy broke off half of the tart and handed it to Jiff.

By the time they'd finished eating, they'd entered the Cardona's property and were immediately confronted by a pair of gigantic mounds of black dirt that seemingly reached into the upper levels of the maple trees that dotted the back yard.

"Wow, they sure look a lot higher close up," remarked Guy, craning his neck to take them all in.

"Race ya to the top!" shouted Jiff, as he set off at a dead run.

"Hey! No fair! You gave no warning!"

But it didn't matter, although his momentum had taken him half way up the side of the tallest pile, Jiff stalled in the loose, cascading soil as he tried desperately to gain footing. Guy was right behind him and together they struggled to reach the crest. At last, their fresh clothes covered in dirt from neck to toe, they scrambled to the top. Trying to keep their balance in the shifting soil, they surveyed the construction site on the other side.

"By the looks of that hole, the house is gonna be a big one," observed Guy.

"Yeah. My father said it's supposed to be done by the middle of the summer."

"That quick?"

Jiff shrugged. "They're in a hurry I guess."

"Wonder if they'll have any kids?"

The implication of Guy's question of course, was would there be any kids their own age in the new household.

Jiff shrugged again. "Hope so. We need new blood around here."

"Is that a dig?"

"'Course not. It's just that it's only you and me right now, not counting Mike. He's too little to count."

While it was true that Mike Dozois was a couple years younger than Jiff and Guy, which at nine years apiece, was like a yawning gap, Guy sometimes felt closer to Mike than Jiff, something he was hesitant to admit even to himself. He and Jiff were supposed to be best friends after all.

"Guess it would be cool to have another kid around," admitted Guy.

Aside from Jiff and Guy and Mike, there were also the "big kids" in the neighborhood including Polly Cardonas' two older sisters and brother and the three Beaudoin boys. Polly's brother Percy and Lewis Beaudoin were the same age, about three years older than Jiff and Guy, but they might as well have been twenty years older from the younger boys' perspective. And insofar as they paid any attention to them, the older guys usually spent their time teasing them or using them for target practice when they felt like throwing a ball around or something. The only time they took them the slightest bit seriously was when they needed warm bodies to play football or stickball.

"C'mon, let's take a closer look at that hole," said Jiff as he began sliding down the opposite side of the dirt mound.

Guy quickly followed.

By the time they reached the bottom, they were filthy both front and back. Brushing off as much of the dirt as they could, they approached the edge of the hole where workmen had already begun preparing the perimeter to receive the concrete forms that would provide the molds for the home's basement level.

"This is going to be a big house," declared Guy, surveying a hole that seemed as big as a football field.

As Jiff began to follow along the edge of the hole, Guy followed, watching loose dirt from their feet as it slid into the hole. They'd rounded a second corner when trucks began to arrive along Burnaby Street on the far side of the dig, some piled high with the wooden forms inside which concrete would pour.

"Hey, you kids!" shouted one of the men as he stepped down from the lead truck. "Get away from there!"

"Yikes!" cried Jiff. "Let's get out of here!"

"Right behind you!"

Scrambling over the lower mounds of dirt, the two boys skidded into the Cardonas' yard and ran across Desrosiers Street to the Jorgenson's. Looking back, they could already see the workmen unloading the wooden forms and sliding them down into the hole.

"That was close," puffed Guy.

"Yeah," agreed Jiff. "Wonder if they'll be pouring the cement today?"

"Hope so," said Guy. "I'd love to see that!"

No sooner than Guy had voiced his hope than a big cement mixer could be seen making its way down Burnaby Street to stop immediately behind the row of trucks already there.

"All riiight!" said Guy. "But they won't be ready to pour for a while. Want to play little army men?"

Re-enacting battle scenes from the movies they saw every Saturday afternoon on TV had become a major pass time for the boys especially after Jiff had received a giant army set the Christmas before. It came with everything necessary to conduct a proper war including both green and grey plastic soldiers (Americans and Germans, natch!), tanks, jeeps, artillery, ruined buildings, and even plastic trees for camouflage. The favorite spot for setting things up was among the shrubbery in front of the Jorgenson's front porch. And as usual for Guy at least, the setting up of the battlefield was the most fun. The actual battle involving taking turns throwing small pebbles at the soldiers by comparison was anti-climactic as the outcome was foreordained: the Americans would win of course!

Thus, the remainder of the morning was spent in happy slaughter of the enemies of freedom until Guy heard his mother calling him for lunch.

"We were done here anyway," said Jiff.

"Next time, you'll be the Germans and I'll be the Americans," said Guy, who thought he'd given a good account of himself before the inevitable defeat.

"Sure, sure," said Jiff but Guy knew that more than likely, Jiff would be the Americans again. It was his army set after all.

"Want to play again after lunch?"

"Nah. Think I'll go down to the Foisy's."

"It's still too cold for swimming," pointed out Guy, hoping to get Jiff to change his mind.

Jiff shrugged, throwing the last piece of the army set into its box. "They're getting the pool ready and I'm gonna see if they need help."

Guy realized that Jiff's altruism was really a way to ingratiate himself with the Foisy's to make sure they kept inviting him down to swim but didn't say so.

But Guy had other alternatives to Jiff if his friend wasn't available. There were Trece and Marie of course. But he'd only consider playing with them if he was desperate. His next younger sister, Rachelle and brothers Joe and Lou were out of the question. That left good ole Mike. Sure, he was two years younger than he was but he seemed advanced for his age. Guy could play with him and the two of them would get along well seemingly more on the same wavelength than even he and Jiff were. Which deep down, bothered Guy at times although he couldn't put the feeling into words.

And so, later that afternoon, he found himself with Mike playing with his Tonka trucks beneath a pair of towering maple trees in his yard. On the front porch, he could hear Trece and Marie playing with Mike's younger sisters.

"Let's extend the road over here and make it go around the tree," suggested Mike, filling a dump truck with dirt.

"Good idea," agreed Guy, pushing a bulldozer and clearing a path toward the tree. "Maybe we can make the road curve in and out of these roots, it'll be more fun to move trucks on a twisty road than a straight one."

"Yeah!"

For the next few minutes the boys were too busy bulldozing and steam shoveling to notice that the blue sky had suddenly clouded over. A late spring chill ran through the air as the world became darker, almost as dark as night.

"Hey, you guys," called Trece from the porch. "I think you'd better come in before it rains."

For the first time, Jiff looked up and noticed the black clouds that had filled the sky.

"You know, Mike, I think she might be right."

"It's cold out," agreed Mike, getting up.

Guy was still thinking whether to go in or not when the rain decided for him.

"C'mon!"

Together, the two boys dashed for the porch steps and barely made it inside before it started to rain, really rain!

For a few minutes it just poured and then, all of a sudden, things changed.

"What's that?" asked Guy, pressing his face against the screens that enclosed the porch. "Looks like little pebbles bouncing all over the street."

"Oh, yeah!" said Mike, crowding up next to him.

The girls were doing the same, all curious at the strange phenomenon.

"Hey, I think those pebbles are getting bigger!"

They were. What began as a rain of pebbles had grown to the size of the marbles in Guy's collection and were bouncing and hopping all over the street and a funny collective hissing sound filled the air.

"It's called hail," said Mrs. Dozois from the door leading from the porch into the house. "Ice forms up there in the clouds sometimes and falls to earth. They're little balls of ice."

"No kiddin'?" said Guy, amazed at the whole phenomenon.

But then, an even more amazing thing happened.

Across Dean Avenue, in the Jorgenson's field, they saw Jiff, back from the Foisy's, running and dashing about with a plastic beach pail in his hand, stooping and picking up things and throwing them in the pail.

"What in the world is he doing?" asked Marie, giggling.

"Hey, Jiff!" called Guy through the window screen. "What are you doin' out there? You nuts?"

Jiff paused only long enough to cup his hand around his mouth and shout back over the noisy hail storm. "I'm fillin' this pail with hail stones! I'm gonna put 'em in the freezer to show my father when he comes home!"

Upon which, he went back to his business as the others watched, still amazed.

"Ya know, that isn't such a bad idea," admitted Mike.

But any thought of going out and imitating Jiff's example was ended when the storm suddenly stopped and the sun came out again. Instantly, the street's wet tarmac, that had so recently been covered in little icy balls, was replaced by a rising mist of steam as the heat of the day destroyed any evidence that the strange storm had happened at all.

By the time Guy and Mike had piled out of the porch and gone outside again, they were only able to find a few of the larger hail stones even as they melted away in their hands.

"Shucks!" said Mike. "We're too late."

"Guess Jiff had the right idea after all," said Guy.

"Kind of wet to go play with the trucks now," said Mike, looking at the muddy mess their construction site had become.

"You guys want to play Sorry?" asked Marie from the porch as if reading their minds.

Guy looked at Mike and shrugged. "Might as well."

The next few weeks passed quickly as school ended and summer vacation began. There was more time for adventures, and playing with little army men and Mike's Tonka trucks, but also games of red light ,and Simon says, and snap the whip. For the latter, the more kids who played the more fun it was and so, Guy, Jiff, and Mike were joined by Trece and Marie, Polly, and Theo Agoulis who lived down at the end of Desrosiers Street where it joined Pleasant. In addition, sometimes, there were Toby and Jeannette Van der Sand.

The brother and sister were babysat by their grandmother who lived on Burnaby Street right across a big, open field next door to the new house being built. They were sometimes seen in the yard and drifted over when they heard the sounds of play on Desrosiers Street. They quickly became part of the group and for Guy and his sisters, proved valuable for one other thing: their own home up past the Dracut Library, had a pool! And so, those days when Jiff left Guy to go swimming at the Foisy's were no longer as hurtful. He and his sisters would often get out their bikes and ride up to the Van der Sands and spend happy afternoons there playing with Toby and Jeannette before finding themselves splashing and laughing in the cool waters of their pool.

But for Guy, the most significant event of the summer would prove a game changer that impacted the whole rest of his life.

It all began one drizzly wet day when he and Jiff were playing on the Jorgenson's front porch.

"Should we leave the ship to explore the Martian surface?" asked Jiff, sitting at the pilot's controls at the end of the porch. The controls of their spaceship were actually some eye screws and short pieces of wood nailed to the banister intended to secure windows in the winter, windows that the Jorgenson's never used and that were stored permanently in their basement. The two boys had just seen the movie *Forbidden Planet* on TV over the weekend that left a deep impression on their fertile minds. They'd been pretending that the front porch was their spaceship and had already visited any number of alien worlds in the meantime. Just now, they'd successfully landed on the planet Mars and were preparing to leave the ship through its airlock which was really the front steps leading down from the porch.

"Looks safe enough," said Jiff, holding his arm out to test the heavy drizzle.

"Maybe it's radioactive?" suggested a wary Guy.

"Might have to put on our spacesuits," said Jiff.

Jiff came up to the airlock himself and looked out over the dreary, overcast world beyond the steps.

"Doesn't look very inviting out there," he observed.

Guy shrugged. "We didn't travel thirty million miles for nothing, did we?"

Guy never did find out what Jiff's reply would have been because just then, they heard someone calling their names.

"Who's that?" asked Guy, looking around.

"Over there," said Jiff, pointing across Desrosiers Street to where Lewis Beaudoin was motioning with his hand for them to come over and join him.

"What does he want with us?" asked Guy, suspicious whenever any of the big kids wanted them for anything. Usually it wasn't for anything good.

"Dunno. Don't see Percy anywhere."

Being the same age, Percy and Lewis hung out together the way Jiff and Guy did. But Percy was nowhere to be seen just then.

"I don't like it," said a wary Guy. "The last time one of the those guy's wanted us it was to play dodge ball and we were always stuck in the middle."

"C'mon," called Lewis. "What's the matter with you guys? I ain't got all day!"

"Might as well see what he wants," said Jiff. "You know if we rile those guys they'll just find something else to bug us with."

"Okay," said Guy, jamming his hat on his head against the drizzle.

A few seconds later, the boys had left the porch at a run, leapt over the front hedges, and approached Lewis who was waiting near the corner of the Beaudoins' property. He wore a baseball cap with his hands jammed into the pockets of his jacket.

"Took you long enough," grumped Lewis.

"Whaddaya want, Lewis," asked Jiff, ignoring the older boy's impatience.

"You asked me once to show you where I buy my comics the next time I went," explained Lewis. "Well I'm goin' now."

The words immediately caught Guy's attention. For the past several weeks he'd been stopping by the Beaudoins' house when he saw Lewis in the yard reading from a stack of magazines. At first, he had no idea what they were, but after being allowed to look through them, he became completely enthralled. They were comic books and their colorful artwork and incredible stories caught his imagination right away, especially those starring super-heroes. And though Lewis had some Superman and Batman comics, it was the ones he called Marvels that seemed to Guy the most visceral. He had to find out where Lewis bought such things!

Discovery of comic books came at exactly the right time for Guy. It was just as he and Jiff found the *Outer Limits* show being rerun on television right after *Fantasmic Features* on Saturday afternoons. Both exposed them for the first time to actual science fiction concepts and ideas. Add to that the occasional airing of various Universal Monsters such as Frankenstein, the Wolf Man, and the Mummy, plus a growing interest in reading that included their voracious consumption of Tom Swift novels they took out from the Dracut Library, and Guy at least, was primed for the next step in the evolution of his imagination.

"Aw, man! Can you wait a minute while I run home? I don't have any money on me," said Guy, who was always broke.

"Me too," said Jiff.

"Well, hurry up!"

Guy didn't have to be told twice. The big kids had little enough patience for the younger children in the neighborhood and he didn't want to try it further. He didn't even wait to discuss the issue with Jiff but just spun about and ran for home as quickly as he could. Now the problem was getting his mother to give him some money. Not always an easy thing to do. For Jiff, it was no problem. If he wanted something, his parents usually got it for him. But for Jiff, his parents were old school; still operating as if it was the Great Depression that they grew up in. As a result, giving out money wasn't second nature to them. Guy usually had to remind them how long it had been since the last time he asked for anything. And this time, he was also under the gun. Lewis wouldn't wait forever!

Dashing up the back steps, Guy burst into the house, almost forgetting to wipe his wet feet on the throw rug by the door.

"Ma!" he called. "Ma!"

"What is it, Guy? No need to shout," said his mother from the pantry.

"You're gonna wake up the babies," warned Trece from the den floor where she and Marie were on their bellies working on a coloring book. Guy barely remembered it was time for his brothers' afternoon naps.

"Ma," said Guy, all out of breath. "Can I have some money to go up to the store?"

Mrs. DeMonde knew it was a dreary day outside, one that had forced the boys to stay inside fending for themselves. Taking pity on her first born, she went to her room to find her purse, Guy following on her heels with hopes rising.

Mrs. DeMonde took the purse from where it hung on a doorknob and fished out her wallet. Snapping open the change compartment, she peered inside and removed a quarter, handing it to an eager Guy.

A whole twenty-five cents! What he could buy for that kind of money!

"*Merci, Maman!*" gasped Guy in profound thanks.

Wasting no time, he ran from the house and back up the street to where Lewis was still waiting.

"My mother gave me a quarter," gasped Guy, still catching his breath.

"That'll get you two comics," said an unimpressed Lewis.

A moment later, Jiff emerged from his house and came over.

"How much did you get?" asked Guy.

"Fifty cents," replied Jiff, holding out a hand to show off the two quarters.

Figures, thought Guy, somewhat resentfully, *Jiff always manages to trump whatever I can get.*

But Lewis had already turned away and begun to lead the way up through the Cardona's yard.

"Where are we goin'?" asked Guy. "This is the way to the library."

"Same direction," said Lewis. "Goin' to Hovey Square Variety."

"I've seen that store when we ride our bikes up to the library," said Jiff. "But we never stopped in."

There was no need to visit Hovey's with Bouchard's right down at the end of Dean Avenue. There, groceries were to be had when mothers sent kids down for a loaf of bread or a quart of milk. Guy liked to go on Friday's when his mother sent him down to pick up fish for supper because the proprietor would let him go behind the deli counter and watch him fry up the fish in big baskets he'd lower into boiling oil. But mostly, the neighborhood kids were drawn to the store because of its vast variety of penny candy. Located at the register just inside the door, the sister of the proprietor would sit and slide back a panel covering the top of a counter and beneath it was revealed dozens of squared off sections each holding a different kind of penny candy. For a dime, children could fill a small paper sack with everything from Bazooka bubble gum to Twizzlers to candy cigarettes. But so far as Guy had ever noticed, they didn't sell comic books.

"That's why I go to Hovey's," said Lewis when Guy had mentioned the fact aloud. "Not only that, but Hovey's has other cool stuff that Bouchard's doesn't have."

"Like what?" asked Jiff.

"You'll see."

By that point, Lewis had led them around the construction site where the new house was being built. There, the concrete forms had long been removed and the wooden structure of the house had risen upon the new foundation. Not only that, but the walls had been enclosed and workmen were busy drywalling the interior.

"They're not wastin' any time with that house, are they?" noted Jiff.

"They want it done by the end of the summer," said Lewis. "I heard that the family's name is Therrien who are gonna be movin' in."

"Any kids?"

"Some. I met one. Name's Butch."

"How old?" asked Guy, who had a bad feeling about anyone named Butch.

"Butch's my age. Funny guy. Think he'll fit in."

"And the others?"

Lewis shrugged. "A sister, Sarah, I think." He shrugged indifference but even Guy could tell he was trying not to show interest.

"I hope they have a younger brother," said Jiff.

"Supposed to be one but I don't know anything about him."

By that point, they'd reached Burnaby Street where Lewis cut through another set of backyards one of which had a heavy rope hanging from a tree. Grabbing hold, he swung out across a steep slope at the bottom of which was a thick thatch of thorn bushes. He made it across easily and swung the rope back to the others.

"You first," said Guy, handing the rope over to Jiff.

"Thanks," replied Jiff, his voice dripping with sarcasm.

He spit in his hands before grabbing the rope, even though the drizzly day had already dampened it. Setting one foot on the side of a big knot tied at the bottom, he prepared to push off.

"Want me to give you a shove?" asked Guy.

"I can make it."

And with that, Jiff swung across as easily as Percy had. Laughing, he sent the rope back to Guy.

"Nothing to it," he called.

Guy had his doubts but there was no way he'd walk around the pit after Jiff used the rope!

Spitting in his hands, he took a good grip on the rough twine, stepped back as far as he could and took a running start. The next thing he knew, he was in the air, swooping across the thorny brush and landing with a solid thud on the other side.

"That was a blast!" he declared when he was sure he was safe. "The people here don't mind you using their swing?"

Percy shrugged. "Dunno. Never see anyone."

In another moment they were on the street again across from a little triangular shaped park with a massive stone monument dedicated to the town's World War I dead. In the distance was another big lot empty but for a lonely stone building in the middle. There was no evidence at all what the building might be used for.

Guy had no time to think about it anyway as they arrived at the entrance to Hovey's. Almost as soon as they entered Percy pointed to the comics where they were displayed in a short wire pocket rack hung at the end of the bread shelves.

"Here they are," he said, immediately plucking a copy of *G.I. Combat*. "I like war comics but for super-heroes, the new Marvels are the most interesting."

Guy had already gathered that from looking through Lewis' collection back home. In fact, he already knew which comics he wanted. Looking through the small selection, he found what he was looking for: the *Amazing Spider-Man*.

It had been easy to spot not only because of its distinctive logo with the webbing against a bright yellow background, but the colorful cover crammed with heroes and villains. Besides Spider-Man himself, there were also the Hulk, the Enforcers, and a new villain called the Green Goblin! Guy grabbed it immediately before either Lewis or Jiff could beat him to it.

He needn't have worried. Lewis was satisfied with his *G.I. Combat* and a copy of *Star Spangled War Stories* and Jiff chose a copy of *Journey Into Mystery* that featured Thor vs the Cobra and Mr. Hyde. A comic Guy would've bought himself if his friend hadn't seen it first. As it was, his second choice was *Tales of Suspense* that had two features for the price of one: Captain America and Iron Man.

It was too early for Guy to realize it, but those first pair of purchases would open the door to a lifelong interest in comic books, one that would prove valuable for those times when he needed perking up.

Right then, however, the delights weren't over yet for he and Jiff as Lewis showed them their next surprise.

"Over here's the toy section," said Lewis, pointing to an alcove set in one of the store's windows, piled high with anything that would catch a child's eye including yoyos, kites, balsa wood airplanes, jacks, marbles, bags of little army men and their accessories, cap pistols and water pistols, games and puzzles and much else.

"Aw, Guy, look at this!" said Jiff, pulling out a box that rattled as he handled it. On its surface was a garishly painted illustration of the Frankenstein monster, just as he looked in the movies they'd seen on Saturday afternoons!

"Wicked! That is so cool!"

"It's a model kit," explained Lewis. "It comes in pieces and you have to put it together with special glue. But the glue doesn't come with the kit. You have to buy it separately."

"No kiddin'!" said Jiff, still in awe at such a find. "How much is it?"

"A quarter ain't gonna do it, that's for sure," laughed Lewis. "And not fifty cents either. These kits go for a dollar apiece."

Jiff whistled, and reluctantly put the model kit back.

"Look here, Jiff," said Guy, pulling out another. "The Hunchback of Notre Dame...and Dracula!"

"They have 'em all!"

"My next birthday, I'm comin' up here to get one!"

"Me too!"

In the meantime, Lewis had pulled out a model of a roadster. "This is what I really came for," he said. "You can have your monsters. I like to build cars. Some day I'm gonna have a real one of my own."

But Guy, at least, wasn't listening. Suddenly exposed to a world of things that up till then he hadn't the slightest idea even existed but now felt that he couldn't live without, suddenly the value of money or the lack of it loomed large in his future plans. It was hard enough to get a nickel or dime from his mother now and then, but how was he to afford items like those model kits that cost a whole dollar? The problem seemed too big to grasp. One thing was for sure: no way was he going to be able to wait until a birthday or Christmas to get one of those model kits! Somehow, he had to find a way to raise the money he needed and already, he had some ideas on the subject.

On the way home, with the drizzle having stopped, Guy began looking through his copy of *Spider-Man* and knew that it was only the tip of an iceberg whose full dimensions he could only guess at. Already, however, something was stirring in his mind. Without quite being able to put his finger on it, he was sure in some deep down level, that he was on the verge of something big. Something like...like...discovering an unknown landscape, one filled with fantasy and adventure that had the potential to go on and on. That could take years or even a whole lifetime to explore! Little did he know that the purchase of those two simple comic books represented the beginning of a journey that would lead him away from the everyday concerns of most other kids his age, one that would never be fully understood by friends and family, but one he couldn't turn back from even if he wanted to.

"Which one of those model kits should we get first, Guy?" Jiff was saying. "The Frankenstein or the Hunchback?"

There was no answer.

"Hey, Guy? I said…"

But Guy, staring at the covers of his new comics, was lost to the world.

CHAPTER THREE

In which Guy and Jiff are amazed

"You still reading that ancient scripture?" teased Dan.

"You should try them sometime," replied Nick, looking up from his hand held viewer. "They're really good and help to pass the time."

Dan shook his head. "Not me. I'm too busy planning for shore leave."

"That's still a couple weeks off."

"All the more reason to get started. We don't want to waste any of that precious time you know."

"We?"

"Sure! We're a team now, you know. Nick and Dan!"

Nick's response was interrupted by the sound of
the shuttle's klaxon. Immediately, the two friends leaped
to their feet and rushed to the nearest observation port.

There, the both gasped in surprise.

Outside, the shuttle was on final approach to
Earthsat 1 where they were due to transship planetside.
But nothing had prepared Nick for its sheer size!

Gateway to the Future
Guy DeMonde

Suddenly, with his discovery of comic books (not to mention
model kits), money became more of an overriding concern for Guy
than it had ever been before. Oh, sure, up to now, he'd been able to
get by asking his mother for a dime here and there for jaunts down
to Bouchard's to buy penny candy, but such an on again off again
dependency would never work for comic books. At twelve cents
each, they were far more expensive than three pieces of Bazooka
bubble gum that could be had for a single penny.

As a result, Guy had to get creative regarding ways to raise the
necessary cash. And since he'd already begun to save the stray soda
pop bottle for its returnable value, it wasn't a stretch to continue
doing that but in a more systematic way.

Already, he'd established a routine. Once a week, he'd grab his
brothers' little red wagon and rattle off to Jiff's house; not to call
him out to play, but on business. There, Mrs. Jorgenson, or
sometimes even Jiff himself, would leave empty pop bottles on the
back porch for him to pick up. Guy couldn't help feeling somewhat
odd about the situation in that here he was scrounging for bottles to
scrape together a few cents to buy comics when Jiff himself only
needed to ask his parents for money and get it. Everything seemed
so easy for Jiff! Guy knew it was mostly due to having only a couple
older siblings to worry about while Guy had five younger ones on
his side, but still, he couldn't help a feeling of embarrassment when

he dropped by to collect bottles and was always relieved to move on afterwards.

His next stop was around the corner on Pleasant Street where there was a little more foot traffic along the sidewalks. There, in a thick patch of lilac bushes, he could always find a few dirty bottles thrown there by passersby. They were usually crawly with ants but a few knocks on the edge of the wagon took care of that.

Next was the real gold mine. At the top of Pleasant Street was Hovey Square Park where local teenagers hung out after dark. There, Guy made his way to the back of the park where a stone wall separated it from some wild woodland on the other side. The teens who hung out back there threw their empty pop bottles toward the wall intending to see them smashed to bits. And though there was shattered glass everywhere on the ground, sometimes bottles would miss the stones in the dark and skitter off into the brush. That's where Guy was now, rooting around there and finding a half dozen bottles still intact.

Now he had a good dozen bottles, the equivalent of twenty-four cents, enough for two comic books!

Arriving at Hovey Square Variety, he stepped into the store's cool interior and set the first group of bottles on the counter.

"I have some bottles to turn in," he told the proprietor who didn't respond, just nodded.

Which was a relief to Guy who could never get used to the man's voice. He'd had an operation on his throat at some point and a device now substituted for his voice. The sound that emerged from the little box in his shirt pocket was creepy and never failed to disturb Guy with its loud, electronic quality.

Quickly, he brought in the remainder of the bottles and waited while the man counted out his money from the cash register. With the comforting weight of the change in his hand, Guy quickly retreated to the comic book rack where he took little time to buy copies of the *X-Men* and *Avengers*. No words needed to be exchanged with the proprietor and he managed to slip out without needing to hear his voice.

Outside, he took the time to examine the covers of his comics, the colorful rendition of the Jack Kirby and Chic Stone art on the cover of the Avengers' encounter with the evil Kang the Conqueror really grabbing his attention. Not that the *X-Men* cover was any less interesting! Again drawn by Jack Kirby, the X-Men battled the Blob while the Brotherhood of Evil Mutants looked on.

But Guy's enthusiasm for Marvel comics had become such that he was compelled to buy all the titles the company produced (well, maybe not *Sgt. Fury and His Howling Commandos*) An expense beyond what he could earn simply by collecting pop bottles. Especially since he'd also begun to collect bubble gum cards; one of the few interests he didn't share with Jiff. He'd discovered them during the waning days of school the previous spring when kids at St. Louis Elementary began showing up with them. Most kids collected baseball cards which didn't interest Guy in the slightest. But others bought cards tied in to popular television shows which *did* grab his interest. Soon, he was dropping by Marie's Variety on the way home from school and buying *Outer Limits* cards, then Batman cards (he wasn't a fan of the company that published Batman, but the cards featured painted images that caught his attention which was quickly being honed to recognize the difference between different artist's styles), *Lost in Space* cards, and the new card set based on Marvel comics characters. The problem with cards though, was that you ended up with a lot of doubles. What to do with them? That problem was solved in the schoolyard where kids would flip their cards against a wall. The owner of the card that came closest to the wall would win all the other cards flipped. As a result, there was always a chance of winning the cards needed to help complete a set. And although buying cards was cheaper than comics being only five cents a pack (for five cards and a stick of gum), for Guy, they nevertheless were a drain on his slim financial resources. Add to that, the occasional penny candy, candy bars, and lunch cakes, and things began to add up.

Eventually, Guy had to admit that pop bottles weren't going to be enough to cover all of his expenses. Another source of income had to be found.

Enter Mr. Softee.

Or rather, his father.

After some tough negotiations, his father agreed to pay him a whole dollar every week to wash the outside of his ice cream truck. All over Lowell, Mr. DeMonde was recognized as the nearest thing to a celebrity the town had. Selling soft serve ice cream, popcorn, and chilleroos, he was known in neighborhoods all over town as Mister Softee.

Which didn't come without some fallout for Guy. Being recognized as "Mister Softee's son" drew unwanted attention his way, and most of it wasn't good. He'd been teased and mocked often in earlier years at school but luckily the kids doing it quickly tired of the practice.

At home, he tried to increase his earnings by asking to also make the chilleroos. These were popsicle-like treats made by filling specially designed Mister Softee cups with flavored water, snapping a plastic cover over the cup, sticking a wooden stick in it, and then placing them in a freezer. The frozen results were one of his father's most popular treats. Unfortunately, the franchise was owned by his sisters who strongly resisted his encroaching on their preserve.

"That's our job," insisted Trece when she heard Guy had asked his father about it. "You wash the truck!"

"Yeah!" agreed Marie. "We want to make money too!"

So much for that idea. But a dollar plus whatever he could haul in for pop bottles was not any inconsiderable amount. For the time being, he was doing okay. Still, it didn't hurt to plan for the future.

"What about a paper route, Pa?" he asked his father one day.

"I can put your name in," said Mr. DeMonde. "But remember, it won't be like working for me. You'll have to be there every single day of the week. Saturdays and Sundays too. Rain or shine."

Guy hadn't really thought about that, but the idea of having all the money he needed for comics and cards and even maybe model kits, was too much of a temptation.

"I understand," he'd replied. "I still want to do it."

"Okay. I'll call the Sun and put your name in."

Later, his father told him that the man who answered the phone said that there was a long wait for routes to become available, especially for specific neighborhoods. Guy was disappointed, but the wait would be worth it.

In the meantime, he was forced to make some hard choices in his comic book purchases: with not enough money to go around, corners had to be cut. As a result, he couldn't buy them all. Besides *Sgt. Fury*, *Tales to Astonish* would soon join the titles he stopped buying (it featured both the Hulk and Sub-Mariner, two characters he didn't care for anyway) and for the rest, he frequently skipped issues. Fortunately, there was an answer for any regrets he had in missing certain comics: his cousin in Salem.

"Let's go and check the comics at Eatons," suggested Guy.

It was a burning hot day in Salem, Massachusetts. Every summer, his parents would drop him off for a week's vacation with his grandparents and his Aunt Blanche who lived with them, but it was really his cousins who lived on the upper floor of the tenement building on Harbor Street that was the real draw. The neighborhood was a middle class one populated mostly by French Canadians living cheek by jowl in closely packed tenement buildings. There weren't any trees in sight except those across the street on the grounds of St. Joseph's Church and its rectory. Otherwise, there was no escape from the sun which beat down unmercifully. Why, there was a picture in the newspaper the other day of a woman frying an egg on the hot sidewalk!

Among his cousins, Paul Montaigne was closest to his own age. A couple years older, he knew the city of Salem like the back of his hand and proceeded to take Guy to all the coolest places like the railroad tracks behind the Parker Brothers toy and game company where they scoured the ground for loose game pieces, or a fur company whose dumpster always had bits of discarded mink or fox scattered around. What they'd do with the bits of fur they found, neither of them had any idea but it was cool to find them. But of most interest to Guy was the fact that Paul knew all the places in town that sold comic books! Around the corner, Gracie's Variety sold used comics for a nickel a piece, and Vallaincourt's Pharmacy had a limited selection under the counter. But Eaton's Pharmacy, as big as any supermarket with a long soda fountain, had a whole spinner rack packed with comics that went back months at a time. But just then, Paul wasn't interested in Eaton's.

"Nah," said Paul to Guy's suggestion. "I know a guy who has tons of comics his mother buys for him and he likes to trade. I want to check out what he has."

"But I don't have anything to trade," protested Guy.

"That's okay, he takes cash too."

Guy shrugged and followed Paul across the graveled driveway (the only backyard the Montaigne's had) to the building next door. There, he ducked into a rear alley and followed a trail that led to another building farther down the street.

"My mother only gave me a dollar to spend," said Guy, who'd hoped to save it to buy a model kit at Almy's department store downtown. He had his eye on a Phantom of the Opera model kit.

"You said you had fifty cents in your pocket," noted Paul arriving at a set of wooden stairs leading onto the ground floor porch of a tenement building. Over a back fence, stretched garage roofs and more tenements and brick apartment buildings that crammed this part of Salem. On the other side lay Ward Street which Guy was warned was populated with punk kids and so to be avoided at all costs.

"I do but I want to go to Gracie's later on," explained Guy.

"Then it's up to you to make the best deal you can, isn't it?"

"Guess so."

"C'mon, then."

Climbing the stairs quickly, the boys reached the third floor landing in good time. Ducking through clotheslines filled with laundry, Paul found the back door and rapped. A moment later, a girl came to the door with a look of disappointment on her face.

"Oh, it's only you," she said. "Vic! Paul's here!"

A lanky kid with the most freckles Guy had ever seen replaced the girl behind the screen door.

"Hey, Paul," he said.

"Hey, Vic. Have any comics you want to sell or trade? This is my cousin Guy. He's here on vacation."

"Sure, I'll get 'em." The boy returned into the darkened interior of the apartment with no special recognition of Guy's presence. Soon, he was back with a big stack of comics that he placed on the floor of the porch. Together the three boys sat around and began going through them.

Although Paul found some war comics he wanted, Guy was disappointed that there weren't any Marvels and said so.

"My mother doesn't like super-hero comics," said Vic. "She thinks their too silly. So she gets me mostly war comics and adventure comics like these *Challengers of the Unknown* and *Sea Devils*."

Though Guy liked the *Sea Devils* covers with their lush wash tones, it wasn't enough to make him part with his valuable quarters. He preferred to wait and see what Eaton's or Gracie's might have had in the way of Marvels.

When they returned home, Paul's sisters asked if they wanted to go swimming with them at Palmer's Cove, a stretch of beach a few blocks from the Montaigne home where Guy had often gone to find clam shells and perriwinkles, snails that clung to the wet stones when the tide went out. The blue water stretched out into a little bay crowded with tethered sail boats and farther along the shore, huge ships filled with coal for the nearby power plant usually sat at anchor. There was also a long wooden pier that older kids used to jump off of into the deeper water of the cove but younger kids like Guy were warned against by parents.

"Well, we were gonna go to Eaton's..." began Guy, but was cut short by Paul.

"Let's go!" he said, turning and heading into the house to put on his bathing suit.

With no choice, Guy did the same.

"Guy, are you sure you want to go barefoot?" asked Claire, the oldest of his cousins.

"Yeah, the sidewalk's gonna be pretty hot," cautioned Celeste, the next oldest.

Guy noted that the girls were barefoot themselves, even Monique who was only a month younger than himself. He figured if they didn't need shoes he didn't either.

"I'm okay," he said, looping his towel around his shoulders.

"You sure?" wondered Claire, looking doubtful.

"You're not wearing any shoes," Guy pointed out.

"Well, we're used to it," said Celeste "We walk there all the time."

Celeste was a favorite of Guy's because she had good taste in reading and often gave him books that he always ended up liking. She'd given him *The Time Machine* by H.G. Wells and *Lord of the Flies* by William Golding both of which he found to be really good so he was inclined to trust her opinion; but not this time.

"Quit bothering me," he insisted. "I'll be okay."

The girls shrugged and the group set off down the driveway and out onto the sidewalk in front of the house. As soon as he began walking on the sidewalk, Guy couldn't help noticing that it was pretty darn hot! But he didn't say anything. By the time they'd crossed Harbor Street and reached the sidewalk on the other side, he was trying to walk more quickly so as to let his bare feet remain in contact with the hot concrete as little as possible. But they'd proceeded down the side street leading to the beach only a short way when it became impossible for Guy to keep walking. His feet were on fire!

"Ow, ow, ow!" he yelled, hopping up and down, trying to keep his feet from burning. Desperately, he looked around for a spot of shade but there was none to be found anywhere on the street. There was no possibility of relief anywhere in sight!

The next thing he knew, the burning had stopped but later, when he had time to think about it, Guy didn't know which was worse, having his feet burn to a crisp or the manner in which he was saved.

Reacting quickly, Claire had scooped him up in her arms and ran back home, only letting him down when they were safely on the back porch. The others were close behind him, including Monique who didn't seem any the worse for wear. He'd never been so humiliated in his life! Not only to be shown up as just plain stupid, but to be rescued and carried home in the arms of a girl to boot!

"We warned you," said Claire when she'd set him down on the cool wooden planking of the porch.

"You should've worn your shoes," said Monique.

"That was great," guffawed Paul. "Never saw anything so hilarious in my life!"

"Don't tease him," said Celeste. "He probably feels pretty horrible already."

It was true. Guy felt so humiliated, he really didn't want to come out again after he'd gone back inside to get his sneakers. But the others waited for him outside so he had to go. Of course, once they reached the beach and the cooling ocean water, all was forgotten...except by Paul who continued to chuckle to himself over the incident.

But it wasn't to be the last unpleasant thing that happened to Guy on his Salem vacation.

He and Paul had spent the afternoon of Guy's last full day of vacation building the models they'd bought at Almy's. Paul had set up a card table on the front porch overlooking the street below and each concentrated on their own projects. Interested in cars, Paul had bought a model of a Ford Fairlane Thunderbolt while Guy had purchased the Phantom of the Opera figure he'd had his eye on. *Wait till Jiff sees this!* thought Guy with satisfaction.

"What do you want to do later?" asked Guy, checking to see if the glue had dried on the Phantom's arms yet.

37

Paul shrugged. "Want to go over to my friend's house and see his model train set-up?"

"Sure!" A model train set-up! That was another thing Guy could only dream of having for his own. It was way too expensive to build up.

"I'll call Hank and see if we can come over," said Paul.

"Is it a big set-up?"

"Big enough to have its own room in the basement."

"Wicked! Can't wait to see it!"

Later that evening, after supper, the two boys walked the couple blocks to Hank's home, a rare, single family house that stood boxed in by tenements. It even had a couple maple trees out front and a bit of lawn in the back.

Instead of going up to the door and announcing himself, Paul led the way down the side of the house to the cellar door. There, they descended a short set of concrete steps. Paul rapped at the door and without waiting for a reply, let himself in.

"Hank? You here?"

"Back here, Paul," came a voice from off in the gloom.

It took Guy's eyes a few seconds to adjust to the light in the basement but before they did, he could tell by the scent of concrete and muskiness that it couldn't be anything but someone's cellar. Gradually, bicycles, storage crates, and a big, fat bellied boiler made themselves apparent. A cleared space from a distant staircase leading upstairs showed the way to a rear area enclosed with two-by-fours stapled over with chicken wire. The room that was thus formed was lit by a fluorescent light that hung from the ceiling together with models of B-52s, Spitfires, and Stuka dive bombers suspended by strings. Guy never saw anything so cool!

"Thanks for letting us come over," Paul was saying.

"No sweat," replied Hank, who was somewhat on the chunky side. "Always like an excuse to show people my set-up."

"This is my cousin, Guy."

"Hi, Guy."

"Hi, Hank," said Guy, giving a little wave. "This sure is a neat set-up! Your own room and everything."

"My dad cleared the area for me and built this cage," explained Hank. "Sort of my own private room. I can even lock the door when I'm not here. Mostly it's to keep the cat from jumping up on the table."

More than ever, Guy wished he could have a set-up like that in his own basement!

"Want to see the trains run?"

"You bet!"

Hank threw a switch on a master control panel and a freight train began to move on the miniature tracks. A "toot toot" sounded from the locomotive along with a puff of smoke from its exhaust.

Guy and Paul laughed at the unexpected sight.

Flipping a second switch, Hank started another train, a passenger train this time, and Guy watched mesmerized as the trains made their ways around a diorama that included mountain tunnels, suburban homes, downtown offices, and rail yards. All of it was dotted with artificial trees, shrubs, and grass. Matchbox cars were stopped at railroad crossings and dump trucks waited to be loaded with sand at an imitation sand pit. Guy thought it all amazing and devoutly wished for the same kind of set-up at home. What fun it'd be to slowly build his own village scene and railroad!

After about an hour in which Hank let Guy control the trains for a while (even raising a drawbridge!), the boys decided to call it quits for the night.

"What do you guys want to do?" asked Hank, locking up the cage.

Paul shrugged. "Want to walk down to Palmer's Cove and see if there's anything going on at the park?"

"Sure."

"What goes on at the park?" Guy wanted to know.

"Stuff. Sometimes there's a softball game going. Or some kids might be throwing a frisbee around. In that case, maybe they'll let us join them for a game."

"It's a nice night out anyway, even if there's no action," said Paul.

"Unless there're girls around," said Hank, nudging Paul with his elbow.

A minute later, they were out of the basement and walking along the street to the cove. Already, Guy could smell the tang of salt water on the heavy air and overhead, a half moon was just coming over the roofs of the tenements. Everywhere, kids were still running about playing hide and seek in the darkening neighborhoods or hopscotch on the sidewalks. In the hot days, the city was mostly quiet but at night, when things cooled down, the streets came alive with activity.

They were almost within sight of the cove when they approached a tenement where a pair of young girls, about Paul and Hank's age, were sitting on the top of the front steps.

"Hiya, boys!" they called.

"Hey, Marsha," acknowledged Hank.

"Is that you, Liz?" asked Paul.

"Who do ya think?"

"Where you guys goin'?"

"To the cove. Wanna come?"

Both girls shrugged at the same time. To Guy's relief, they didn't seem interested.

"Who's that with you," asked Marsha, nodding in Guy's direction.

"My cousin, Guy."

"He's cute. I think." said Marsha.

"Come a little closer, Guy," beckoned Liz.

The boys moved in to where the streetlight lit their features.

"Hey, you're right, Marsha. He is cute."

"Come here and sit with us for a minute," invited Liz as she scooted over a little to make room between she and Marsha.

Guy looked questioningly at Paul, suddenly filled with an unaccountable nervousness.

"Go on," said Paul. "Let 'em get it outta their system."

Guy, unwilling to let on that he was as nervous as he felt and aware of his embarrassing rescue earlier in the week when Claire had to carry him home to keep his feet from burning, plunged boldly ahead.

Mounting the stairs two at a time, he plunked himself down between the two girls who, now that he could see them close up, were uncomfortably attractive.

"Relax, Guy, we don't bite," cooed Marsha, shoving him playfully with her shoulder.

"Oh, he isn't nervous, are you Guy?" said Liz, giving his crewcut a playful rub.

"Of course not," said Guy, trying to keep the quaver out of his voice. The two girls smelled pleasantly of fresh soap and shampoo. All of a sudden, he felt strangely over heated and broke out into a sweat. He tried to wipe his damp palms against his shirt hoping nobody would notice.

"Oh, good!" said Marsha as both girls suddenly leaned in and kissed him on both cheeks at once!

Instantly, as if charged with a jolt of electricity, Guy leaped from where he was sitting clear over all the steps to land squarely on the sidewalk below.

At the same time, everyone burst out laughing at his predicament as Paul and Hank thumped his back and gave him good natured shoves.

"Why, Guy, was it all that bad?" teased Liz, laughing.

"You'd think we bit him or something," said an amused Marsha.

"Did you see how far he jumped?" laughed Hank. "He could qualify for the Olympics!"

"Don't worry, Guy," soothed Paul as they continued on their way. "They do that to any new guy that comes into the neighborhood. You should be flattered."

Flattered wouldn't be the word a mortified Guy would have used just then however. Two humiliating instances within a few days of each other was more than his bruised ego could take. He'd always enjoyed and looked forward to spending a whole week with his cousins in Salem before, and would again he was sure, but just at the moment, he decided that he'd had enough. Now, he looked forward to going home the next day. It would be a relief to be back on Desrosiers Street and back among his friends!

And so, a few days later, he found himself once more in the cozy, comfortable surroundings of Desrosiers Street but contrary to his expectations, the comfort of familiarity was lacking and took some days more to recapture. In short, after being gone for over a week, it felt strange to be back home. His friends had found ways to distract themselves without him being around and upon his arrival, were all busy doing those other things. Left at loose ends, and feeling somewhat sorry for himself, Guy decided that he needed to be alone for awhile, a feeling that came over him from time to time even if he hadn't been away. When that mood came upon him, he liked to retreat to the woods and fields at the end of Desrosiers Street that were bounded by Beaver Brook on the south side and the Merrimack River in the east where the brook eventually emptied.

At first, he found his way to the top of a big hill that dominated the wild area, a hill he decided to name Lookout Hill which gave a grand view of the Merrimack in the distance and the Centralville section of Lowell that hugged its banks. From where he stood, he could clearly make out the red brick pile that was St. Louis School and the fire station tower. On the top of a rise to the north, there was a big old mansion that looked deserted and that Guy liked to imagine might be haunted.

Tired of the view but not ready to head home, he made his way down the reverse slope of the hill in the direction of Beaver Brook. Forcing his way through grass as tall as he was, he headed for the sound of rushing waters. Finally, he broke through to the brook and found himself beneath a gnarly old maple tree that swayed in the slight breeze. For a moment, Guy simply stood, closed his eyes, and listened to the sound of the wind rustling the leaves in the tree. When he opened them again, he was staring up into the branches and immediately recognized a perfect spot for a tree house. *Yeah,* he thought, *I could nail a few boards across those branches and then lay some logs across 'em and make a nice platform!*

The more he thought about it, the more he liked the idea. It would be the perfect place to come when he wanted to be alone. Or just to read without his siblings breaking his concentration. He pictured himself sitting way up there in the tree, the brook running beneath him, the blue sky overhead, and dreaming, or thinking up stories that he'd begun to think of writing, or even dozing in the warm, dappled sunlight that managed to make its way through the tree's thick canopy of leaves. Excited by his imaginings, he turned for home, already with a plan about where he might be able to get some wood for the project.

By late the next afternoon, the platform was finished. As expected, it was an easy job to talk old Mr. Leblanc into letting him have the few two-by-fours he needed for the frame of the platform. Mr. Leblanc was a contractor who cut and milled his own lumber using big saws and planers that filled his garage on Lupine Road. Often, when Jiff wasn't around, Guy would spend time over there watching Mr. Leblanc shove raw lumber into his machines and turn them into finished boards. Sometimes, he'd take a broom and sweep up the piles of sawdust that filled every space in the garage.

With a hammer, hand saw, and a pocketful of nails taken from home, he'd made his way to the tree he found and set to work. First, he nailed some short pieces of wood against the tree trunk to use as hand and foot holds. Then, once he was able to crouch on the branches he had in mind for the frame, nailed the two-by-fours, one at a time, in a rough square from one branch to another. It didn't take long to find fallen branches in some nearby woods and, cutting them into pieces, nailing them across the two by fours forming the platform. Finally, he cut a square opening in the floor pieces near the tree trunk so that when he climbed the wooden steps, he'd emerge onto the platform through the hole. In a last minute inspiration, he'd taken some leftover branches and nailed them around the platform about waist high to form a safety rail of sorts. Now, standing on the platform, testing its strength by jumping up and down, he was more than satisfied with his work. He finally had a place all his own. And, surprising himself, decided he wouldn't tell anyone about it, not even Jiff. But immediately upon thinking such a thing, he wondered what it meant. Was Jiff his best friend or not? If he was, wasn't he obligated not to keep any secrets from him? He wasn't sure what it meant, but he knew he wanted a place just for his own. A retreat that no one else knew about that he could be sure when he ventured there, whatever dreams he dreamed there, would be only his.

It was a week later and Guy had recovered from his funk and reintegrated himself in the doings of the neighborhood. While he'd been gone, the workers had finished the new house off Burnaby Street and the new owners moved in. Lewis had been right. There were children in the family including Butchy, the oldest, and Sarah his younger sister. And to Jiff and Guy's delight, the youngest Therrien sibling was a boy named Don. It was true he was only about Mike's age but it didn't matter. His enthusiasm and high spirits as well as his native intelligence (whatever that was; it was a phrase Guy had encountered in his reading) made him a natural addition to the neighborhood's younger set. From that point, Jiff and Guy went from being a twosome to a threesome or even a foursome if Mike was counted. And if Don was, then Mike had to be too. What's more, Don turned out to be the connecting fiber between the big kids in the neighborhood and the younger kids. With his older brother joining Lewis and Percy, now the big kids might count on recruiting Jiff and Guy and their friends to make teams for games of stickball and football. Which sometimes didn't help Guy much as for some reason, the big guys chose to tease him. Why that was, Guy didn't understand. Maybe it was because he just wasn't that good at sports or something. What hurt more though was that sometimes Jiff would join them in the teasing.

And so, from that time on, there seemed to be an invisible wall going up between he and Jiff. Those early days when it was just the two of them were gone forever and now Guy had to share his best friend with others. He liked Don and Mike as he did Jiff, but the dynamic between them had changed in a way that Guy couldn't figure out.

It was a subtle thing to be sure. One that only troubled Guy deep in the back of his mind. However, it was something he never let on and for the time being, it seemed that the neighborhood gang had been completed. With Jiff and Guy plus Mike and Don, there was no need for anyone else to join their group. If they needed more people for a good game of kick the can or Great Escape, there was always Trece and Marie, Polly Cardona, and Theo Agoulis and even Toby and Jeannette Van der Sand to fill out the ranks.

But they were wrong.

One day, Guy was surprised to see Jiff at his back door, breathless after having run all the way over from his house.

"What's up?" asked Guy.

"You…" Jiff paused to catch his breath. "…gotta see this!"

"See what?" asked Guy with rising excitement. No way Jiff would be acting like this over nothing!

"You gotta see it to believe it!"

"See what?"

"You'll see! Hurry up! You're not gonna believe it," gasped Jiff, repeating himself.

Hurrying to his room, Guy threw on some clothes and ran outdoors not even pausing to tell his mother that he was going out.

"What's the matter?" asked Guy as Jiff fairly pulled him along by his arm.

"Hurry! We don't wanna miss it!"

Jiff began to run and Guy found himself huffing and puffing to keep up with him but finally his friend came to an abrupt halt at the top of Dean Avenue and there, before his unbelieving eyes, Guy saw the most incredible sight he'd ever seen coming up Desrosiers Street!

CHAPTER FOUR

In which Jiff and Guy are scandalized

Around them, the bar was a shambles.

Nick and Dan stood back to back, exhausted, their cadet uniforms torn and dirty.

"Had enough?" challenged Dan to the ring of onlookers not knocked unconscious and lying on the floor with the others.

"Take it easy, Dan," warned Nick, holding his fists up, ready for the next onslaught. "We're outnumbered you know."

"Well, I'm upping the odds," said a strange voice.

Nick and Dan both turned to see another cadet, one they had not seen before, step to their side and raise his own fists.

"Who are you?" asked Nick, amazed.

"Troy," said the stranger. "But you can call me Buster."

Together, the threesome turned to face their challengers who began to think twice and ease off.

"Drinks on the house!" shouted Buster, sensing the change in mood.

Gateway to the Future
Guy DeMonde

It was the most amazing thing Guy had ever seen.

The most amazing thing any of the kids gathered there had ever seen.

"What'd I tell ya?" asked Jiff, pointing. "Ever see anything like that?"

Guy shook his head, his mouth open in awe.

"Even though my father told us something like this was gonna happen, I didn't really believe it," said Jiff.

"Me neither. It's one thing to hear him tell about it, but another to actually see it."

Around them now, at the top of the hill where Dean Avenue and Desrosiers Street met, everyone in the neighborhood had gathered to see the incredible sight that was slowly approaching them, coming uphill in their direction.

Of course, Mr. DeMonde and Mr. Jorgensen, as well as all the other fathers in the neighborhood were gone to work, but mothers were standing on the sides of the road and all the kids around were there too, even school mates Guy knew from St. Louis who lived on Tilden Avenue were there, and kids he and Jiff sometimes palled around with from off Pleasant Street, and even Skip and his friends from Burnaby Street that Lewis and Percy knew couldn't stay away.

"How do you think they did it?" asked Guy.

"Don said that his father told him they punch holes in the basement and then slide steel beams under it," explained Jiff. "Then they use hydraulic lifts to get it high enough for the truck to get under it."

"Man! We should've gone over to see that," said Guy.

"If only we'd known they were gonna do it today!"

"Waddaya think?" asked Don after dashing across the street to join the others. "Didn't I tell ya?"

"Your father was right," admitted Jiff.

"But how are they gonna get it off the truck?" asked Mike, who'd been standing with Guy and Jiff all along, too amazed to say anything till then.

And the sight *was* incredible. Sitting on top of a big, flatbed truck was a two story house! It was a duplex with separate apartments on either end and colored a sickly shade of green.

"That's one ugly house," noted Jiff.

"That's gonna go right next door to me?" wondered Guy, not at all sure if he liked the idea. "It'll block the view from our house to yours."

"I hadn't thought of that," admitted Jiff.

For the last several weeks, the boys had known where the house was to be located because the empty lot on the corner of Dean and Desrosiers Street, directly across from the Jorgenson's had been prepared for it. Although a full basement hadn't been installed, a foundation made of concrete blocks mimiced the outline of the house. Plumbing and other utilities had been installed ready to be attached once the house was settled over the foundation.

Guy already knew his mother wouldn't like it either. With such a towering monstrosity blocking the view to the rest of the neighborhood, she wouldn't be able to see what Guy and his sisters were up to when they were with their friends.

Traffic on Pleasant Street had been blocked by the police earlier that morning when transport of the house had begun. And now a police car, its emergency light flashing, was slowly preceding the hauler up Desrosiers Street.

"Why are they even bothering to move that house here?" asked Guy, suddenly concerned that the new house wouldn't fit in with the rest of the neighborhood. "Why didn't they just build a new house and leave that old one where it was?"

Jiff shrugged. "Maybe they like our neighborhood better. I would."

"My father said that they're gonna build a new house on the old lot and it was cheaper to move the old house here," said Don as the police car reached them and the big flatbed truck inched close enough so that they could see every detail of the house.

"Look at how all the pipes stick out underneath," observed Guy, stooping to get a better look at the rafters and flooring underneath the house. Overhead, at such close range, the building towered hugely over their heads.

"Ooooh, yeaaaah," said Jiff, doing the same.

"And all those cobwebs," said Mike, pointing. "Yech!"

Alongside the house, a team of workers escorted the load, keeping a sharp eye out for anything that might upset the balance but so far it had all appeared to be a smooth operation. Eventually, the parade reached its destination and a slow, slow process began to position the flatbed such that the truck could back up onto the lot and over the prepared foundation wall. But it all was taking so much time that even the boys grew impatient. By then, most everyone had seen enough and left and only a few stragglers remained.

"I'm getting' hungry," said Mike.

"Me too," said Don. "Must be almost lunch time."

"It's taking too long for them to finish," said Jiff. "I'm going home to eat. Maybe they'll be done after lunch."

"Hey, I got a good idea," said Guy. "Why don't we eat our lunches outside at your picnic table and we can keep watching what they're doing from there?"

Jiff shrugged. "Okay. Meet you there."

Going home, Guy informed his mother of he and Jiff's plans so she wrapped the Fluffernutter sandwich she'd previously prepared for him in wax paper and filled an empty peanut butter jar with milk. Adding a Scooter Pie to the ensemble, she packed it all into a brown paper bag and handed it to Guy.

"You make sure to stay away from those workers," she warned. "Watch from across the street."

"Yeah, ma," said Guy in a bored tone.

Already, he was getting a good idea of what it was going to be like having that big, two story house right next to them. Looking out the pantry window, where he once could see Jiff's house plainly across Dean Avenue, now it was dominated by the new building that just then was hovering over its foundation blocks waiting for the workers to arrange the hydraulic lifts underneath to raise it off the truck and allow the truck to pull out. Because of its size, it seemed a whole lot closer than it really was. How would his family ever get used to it being there?

Outside, the summer sun was still shining down from a cloudless blue sky. But somehow, whatever delight Guy might have felt in it was robbed at the sight of the house being slowly lowered onto its foundations next door.

Warily, he skirted the work area and the wooden barricades thrown up around the site by the workers and reached Jiff's front yard. In another minute he was skipping down the stone steps next to the brick fireplace that led down to the Jorgenson's back yard. There, the others had already gathered at the picnic table beneath a huge, spreading maple tree that dappled the area in cool shade.

"Took you long enough to get here, Guy," said Jiff, a ham and cheese sandwich resting on his crushed brown bag.

"I had the farthest to go," returned Guy, finding his place next to Jiff. Across the table from them sat Mike and Don who were just then taking the first bites out of their sandwiches.

"Think they'll finish with that house today?" asked Don, craning his neck in the direction of the house.

Jiff shrugged. "They're moving pretty fast now. It's almost the whole way down."

"Not gonna like it there," said Guy, still in a gloomy mood over the whole business.

"Me neither," agreed Mike, whose home was also right next door to the new house.

"Yeah, I won't be able to see your house anymore, Guy," said Jiff.

It seemed that the new house was symbolic in some way. Like it physically represented whatever it was Guy felt was coming between himself and his best friend. For that reason, Guy would never reconcile himself to its presence. He'd always hate it.

"What you got for dessert?" Don asked no one in particular.

"Twinkies," said Jiff, holding up the package of twin golden cakes.

"Ring Ding," said Mike. "Giant sized."

"Trade ya for it," said Guy quickly.

"Whadaya got?"

"Scooter Pie."

"You kiddin'? For a Ring Ding?"

"It's one of those new strawberry flavored Scooter Pies."

"Nothin' doin'!"

Jiff laughed. "He's wisin' up, Guy!"

It was true. Some of Don's "native intelligence" had been rubbing off on Mike recently. Though both Don and Mike were a couple of years younger than Guy and one younger than Jiff, the gap had almost fully disappeared by that point until no thought was given to anything they all did together.

"Wonder who'll end up livin' there?" said Don.

"You mean kids?" asked Mike.

"Yeah. Wonder if this time next year, we'll have someone else sittin' with us here havin' lunch?"

Guy had never thought of that possibility.

"Could be," mused Jiff, taking a drink from his thermos.

Guy, starting in on his Scooter Pie, wondered if he could ever accept anyone from that house as a friend?

It was only a few weeks later that he was due to find out.

He and Jiff were playing little army men among the hedges that bordered the Jorgenson's front yard. The edge of the road there was unpaved and given over mostly to sand allowing for easy digging. It was about mid-morning but the sun overhead was already hot and threatened another "Foisy day" for Jiff that afternoon. Guy tried to keep that eventuality out of his mind and concentrate on having fun with his friend as they set up the army set in their best approximation of the movie they'd seen the previous Saturday afternoon: *The Sands of Iwo Jima*.

"I don't remember any jungles on Iwo Jima," said Guy, concerned that they'd set up some of their men among the hedges instead of restricting the action to the sandy area next to the road.

"There was some at the beginning of the movie," countered Jiff.

"I don't know," said Guy. "I don't think that was Iwo Jima. I think it was Tarawa."

"Huh? How do you know about...?"

"Tarawa. It was another island where we fought the Japs before Iwo Jima. I read it in a book."

Guy didn't bother mentioning the book was *The Story of World War II,* one he bought from the Scholastic Book Club at school. Written in an engaging style with plenty of descriptions of personal heroism, Guy found it so thrilling that he'd begun to take out more books about World War II from the library.

Jiff thought a moment. "You might be right. Maybe we should have a two part war then? We do the battle of Tarawa up here in the hedges and then Iwo Jima down here in the sand?"

"Good idea," agreed Guy as he continued to mold sand into pill boxes, berms, and foxholes for his troops. Naturally, he was the bad guy again and Jiff the Americans.

They were both concentrating so much on setting up their men that they never noticed it when Chuck came over.

He was almost bleached blond with short, curly hair and he was obviously no older than either Jiff or Guy. But there was something self-assured about him, more worldly. And he wasn't shy at all upon meeting anyone new.

What'cha doin?" he asked.

Startled at the sound of the voice, Jiff and Guy snapped around in its direction.

"Playin' with our army men," explained Jiff, after a brief appraisal of the newcomer. "Who're you?"

As he spoke, Jiff rose to his feet. Guy was right behind him.

"Name's Chuck," said the boy, who stood with his hands jammed into the pockets of his jeans. "Chuck Lavalle. Just moved in over there."

He threw his head back in the direction of the new house, the side that faced Desrosiers Street.

"We saw that house when it came up the street," said Guy. "When did you move in?"

"Couple days ago," said Chuck. "Me, my big brother, and my dad."

"And your mother," finished Jiff.

Chuck shook his head. "She don't live with us."

"Huh?" Jiff and Guy exchanged looks of consternation.

"They're divorced, my mom and my dad. Me and my brother live with my dad."

Jiff and Guy were temporarily speechless. Divorced? They'd never heard of such a thing. Not in real life anyway. Just like the aliens they saw on the *Outer Limits*, divorce was just as unbelievable. Guy would have felt mortified for Chuck having people know about such a shameful thing, but the boy didn't seem to mind.

"Divorced? Really?" asked Jiff, still not quite believing what he'd heard.

"Sure. No big deal." Chuck leaned over and spit into the sand. "Don't go to church either."

That news doubled Guy's shock. Never in his ten years had he ever dreamed of actually encountering such scandals!

"Don't go to church?" he asked, stunned.

He'd known that sometimes Jiff didn't go to church every Sunday but he wasn't Catholic after all. But everyone else Guy had ever known was.

"Nah. My dad says that he went enough times when he was a kid so that he doesn't need to go anymore."

While Jiff paused to consider the logic of the statement, Guy remained scandalized, unable to understand such strange logic.

"So you playin' army?" asked Chuck, lifting his chin in the direction of the boys' troop dispositions.

"Yeah, we're doin' the battle of Iwo Jima," replied Jiff. "Ever see the movie *Sands of Iwo Jima?*"

Chuck shook his head. "Missed that one."

"Wanna play with us?" asked Guy.

Chuck shrugged and spit again. "Nah. How 'bout playin' pitcher and catcher instead? With three guys, we can go to the park and hit some around too. I got a new first basemen's mitt."

"Okay!" agreed Jiff.

"But what about our set up?" pleaded Guy. "We're almost ready to start the fight."

"I'd rather go to the park," said Jiff. "Besides, it's my army set and if I don't want to play, we'll put it away."

Guy was disappointed. He'd rather play army than baseball but had no choice in the matter. Suddenly, he wished that Mike or Don had been around. He was sure they'd have sided with him and Jiff would have yielded.

Quickly, he helped Jiff pack up the set and went home to get his baseball glove. Together, the trio walked up to Hovey Square Park to play on the little league field there, taking turns at bat and pitching and fielding. Guy enjoyed it but not as much as he would have finishing the battle of Iwo Jima.

"C'mon, Guy!" called Chuck from home base where he stood waiting for Jiff to throw the ball. "Stop daydreaming!"

"I'm not daydreaming," said Guy, even though he was.

"Here comes one," shouted Chuck, pointing with the bat like Babe Ruth to the edge of the outfield where woodland began.

"Talk's cheap!" shouted Guy back at him.

Suddenly, there was a crack and Guy barely had time to pounce after the bounding ball. He closed his eyes at the last minute, afraid he'd miss it but he felt the comforting thump in the basket of his glove and when he opened his eyes, there was the grass stained baseball.

"Damn!" said Chuck, throwing the bat aside as they rotated positions.

Again, Guy had been scandalized when he'd heard Chuck swear for the first time. No one he knew ever used such language. Not even Percy or Lewis. Certainly not kids their age. If they did, he shuddered to think what their parents would do if they ever heard them using such words. Between his spitting and swearing and his divorced parents and not going to church, Guy began to wonder about how much different Chuck's life had been than his own. But as strange as he could imagine it, it wasn't strange enough to keep him from feeling a fascination for his new friend. There was something of the exotic and new about him that was attractive and exciting in a forbidden sort of way. And though Guy could never bring himself to use the kind of colorful language Chuck did, by the time they'd left the park, he and Jiff were both spitting just like he was.

CHAPTER FIVE

*In which Guy makes new friends
and fights for his honor*

"I'll hold your coat while you show him who's boss," said Buster, helping Nick off with his cadet dress jacket.

He, Dan, and Buster were in attendance at the cadets' formal graduation ball and inside the chapter house, all was brilliant lights, music, and dancing couples. But outside, it was dark in the commandant's garden, with its high shrubbery blocking the view from inside the chapter house.

A fellow cadet had insulted the form in which Nick, Dan, and Buster were members and when that happened, everyone knew the rules: the insult needed to be wiped away usually with fisticuffs.

"Thanks," said Nick, shrugging out of his jacket.

"You can take him," snarled Buster. "He's nothing but hot air."

"We'll see about that," said the insulter's second.

"Keep your guard up," whispered Dan in his ear. "He favors his left but I heard he has a glass jaw."

Nick nodded and raised his fists.

Gateway to the Future
Guy DeMonde

"This here's Chuck," Jiff was saying as he introduced the newcomer to Don and Mike.

"The kid who moved into that house that came up the street?" asked Don, looking Chuck over.

"That's right," said Chuck, spitting.

"Hi ya, Chuck," greeted Mike good naturedly.

Chuck looked the two of them over. "These guys are kinda little to be hangin' around with you and Guy, Jiff," he said.

"Hey!" said Don.

"Yeah! Whadaya mean by that?" demanded Mike, his good nature suddenly evaporating.

"Just what I said," replied Chuck.

"Relax, Chuck," soothed Jiff. "Don and Mike are all right. You'll see."

Guy said nothing, contenting himself with looking over the situation and not liking it. Chuck had no call for hurting his friends' feelings.

Chuck shrugged.

Just then, the big kids came out of Don's house: Lewis, Percy, Butchy, and Sarah. Trundling noisily down the wooden stairs leading down from the Therrien's back door, they skidded along an earthen slope from where a concrete walkway lined the back of the house. At the bottom, where Guy and his friends were waiting, was a wide, circular patch of bare earth in the center of the lawn, worn smooth from weeks of play.

Ever since the Therriens had moved in, their backyard had quickly become the nexus of much of the activity in the neighborhood. Because the backyard was not only adjacent to the Cardonas' and Beaudoins' properties, but was located alongside a big, open field that separated the Therrien property from the house where Toby and Jeannette Van der Sand's grandmother lived, it was perfect for playing stickball. After dark, with the spotlights at the corners of the house lit, the area was made for games of kick the can as children could hide in any number of places and, just outside the rings of light cast by the spotlights, could approach the can without being seen.

Just now, however, the big kids had summoned them for a game of stickball.

"You guys ready?" asked Lewis, swinging the bat, which was nothing more than a cut down broom handle.

"We been waitin' for an hour for you guys," said Jiff.

"Don't give me any of your sass, Jiff," said Butchy, tossing a spongeball up and down in his hand.

"Knock it off, Butch!" said Don, unafraid of his older brother. Likely due to the fact that he had an infirmity that required he wear a big, elevated shoe on one foot. Guy was positive that their parents wouldn't look too kindly on Butch if he pushed Don around too much. Not that Don needed much defending. He was the best athlete among his friends making catches and plays that truly astounded everyone.

"Keep quiet, squirt," said Butch.

"Let's choose sides," said Sarah, eager to play.

"Okay, okay," said Butch, tossing the bat to Percy. "Lew, you want to be the other captain?"

"Yeah."

It was a given that Guy and his friends were automatically out of the running for captain so no one in that quarter raised any objections.

Percy had caught the bat near the bottom on purpose so as to give plenty of room for the hand over hand method he and Lewis used not only to see who would be up first, but who would get first choice in picking sides. As he'd planned, it was Percy's hand that capped the process.

"All right!" said Percy gleefully, immediately choosing Butchy for his team.

Lewis chose Sarah next. Besides being pretty, she could play better than any of the younger kids except maybe Don.

"Jiff, get over here," said Percy.

There was a clear spring in Jiff's step as he joined Percy's team. Everyone knew at that point which team would end up being the strongest.

"I'll take Chuck," returned Lewis.

"Don," said Percy.

"Mike," said Lewis, his voice indicating that they were scraping the bottom of the talent pool at that point.

"I guess we're stuck with Guy," said Percy. "Unless you want him?"

Lewis considered the relative strengths of the two teams.

"Guess we'll take him," he finally said. "We can use more people in the infield."

Guy walked over to Lewis' team without much enthusiasm and not without a little embarrassment.

"You take the outfield, Guy," ordered Lewis. "Not much damage you can do out there."

There was nothing new about Guy being chosen last. He was always last to be chosen. The fact was, he just wasn't that good at sports. Unlike Don, he wasn't that coordinated and anyway, couldn't muster up the enthusiasm that made good plays possible.

"Sarah, you pitch and I'll play shortstop," instructed Lewis.

"Right," replied Sarah, already understanding that most of the hits using a sponge ball wouldn't extend much beyond the infield.

"Chuck, you take first base," said Lewis, pointing at the fence post that anchored the Beaudoin's back yard. "And you better not miss it when we throw the ball to you."

"I won't," assured Chuck, pounding his first baseman's mitt with a fist.

"Mike, second base," said Lewis.

While these dispositions were being made, a resigned Guy trudged to the outfield which was located far out in the field adjoining the Therrien's property. As soon as he cleared the shade of the trees, the sun beat down unmercifully on his bare head. Finally, so far out that the other players seemed only tiny figures in the distance, Guy turned and shaded his eyes against the sun's glare, hoping that no one hit the ball in his direction.

"Ready?" called Lewis to his team mates. He didn't bother to check with Guy.

When everyone signaled their readiness, Sarah underhanded the first pitch to Percy.

He had to have hit the ball just right because it not only cleared the infield, but sailed far out into the outfield! Guy craned his neck to watch the ball as it rose higher and higher into the air but then lost it in the bright sunlight. He held out his glove where he guessed the ball might fall and tried to blank out the shouts of the others as they both encouraged him to succeed and groaned that it would be a sure home run for Percy.

As it turned out, the latter were right. The ball hit the ground a dozen feet from where Guy had expected it and bounced across the grass way off with Guy chasing after it with all his might. The others were still screaming at him to hurry up and throw the ball back so he knew Percy hadn't yet rounded all the bases. Winding up, he threw the ball as hard as he could but it wasn't good enough. It fell way short of Butch who had run out to shorten the distance and by the time he managed to snag it, Percy had crossed home plate to the cheers and jeers of his team mates.

"Attaway, Guy!" shouted Percy, laughing.

It was bad enough that the big guys laughed at him, but it was worse when Jiff joined them.

"We can always count on you, Guy!" Jiff was calling around his cupped hands.

That jibe hurt Guy the most. Jiff was his best friend, but sometimes when they played with the big kids, he couldn't help wanting to be accepted by them, more than he cared about being Jiff's friend it seemed. Once away from them, Jiff would revert to his usual self but that didn't make Guy feel any better.

Slowly, he returned to his position in the outfield to await the next humiliating moment.

And so, the afternoon wore on. The innings came and went and once Guy even hit a double and was hit home by Chuck, surprising everyone. For a brief few minutes, he'd redeemed himself and had the secret satisfaction of watching Jiff scramble to field the ball and then fumbling it. But the end was a foregone conclusion. The teams proved fairly balanced with Percy and Butch backed up by Jiff and Don on one team and Lewis and Sarah on the other. The action see sawed back and forth until Percy's team finally won.

"No thanks to Guy," teased Jiff.

"I got that double!" shot back Guy.

The group was sprawled on the steep, shady slope leading up to the wall surrounding the Therrien's house. Sarah had retreated indoors for a drink.

"You were lucky."

"But it came in handy," admitted Lewis.

"Too bad he couldn't play like that more often," said Butch.

"They all need to be faster running the bases," observed Lewis.

"Yeah, they need to get more running time in," said Percy.

"What they need is some inducement," said Butch.

"Whadaya mean?" asked Don, wary of his older brother.

Butch sprung to his feet and signaled for Percy and Lewis to join him in the bare patch at the foot of the slope.

"What these kids need is more practice running," he said. "More judgment in when to steal a base and when to go back."

"Yeah, go on."

"Hey, you guys," said Butch to the younger kids. "Get up there on the wall by the back steps. Go on."

Uncertainly, Jiff, Guy, Don, Mike, and Chuck did as Butch said.

"Now then, one at a time, you guys run along the wall while I try to hit you with the ball. Try to make it to the other end without being hit."

"I get it," said Lewis, smiling.

Guy and Jiff looked at each other but before they had a chance to decide if it was a good idea, Chuck dashed off. Immediately,

Butch threw the sponge ball with all his might. Chuck halted in his tracks and let the ball bounce off the basement wall and then continued to the other side arriving there safely.

"Piece of cake," he called to the others, then spat.

Following suit, Jiff spit and started running.

This time, Lewis whipped the ball well ahead of Jiff and timed the throw perfectly, hitting Jiff in the thigh. "Ow!" cried Jiff, before half limping the rest of the way, but slow enough to give Percy a chance at another throw that barely missed his head.

"Man, that stung!" said Jiff, spitting.

"Comin' Guy?" challenged Chuck.

Guy wasn't wild about the idea but of course, he had no choice. If he refused, he'd lose the respect of his friends and besides, he couldn't let Jiff do anything he wouldn't do.

"C'mon, Guy," said Percy. "We haven't got all day!"

Percy hadn't finished his taunt when Guy launched himself along the wall, running as fast as he could.

"C'mon, Guy!" urged Jiff.

"You can make it," called Mike.

Guy was only half way when he saw Percy's arm pull back. His timing was good because he stopped short, crediting his Keds for the save, allowing the ball to strike the basement wall well ahead of him. But as he started up again, Butch had grabbed the ball on the rebound and wasted no time in throwing it again. But his throw was too hasty and the ball struck the side of the house far over Guy's head. By then, it was too late for a third try and Guy was safely on the other side, panting to catch his breath and proud that he'd bested Jiff by not being hit.

"Great run, Guy!" congratulated Chuck, thumping him on the back.

"Yeah, lucky you didn't get hit like I did," said Jiff, still smarting.

Next was Don's turn but he wasn't as lucky as Guy or Chuck. He was hit in the side, lost his footing and fell. By the time he was able to regain his feet again, he'd been hit another couple times before finally stumbling to the other side.

Mike fared almost as bad and Guy could tell he wanted to cry but managed to control himself.

The game continued for a while longer until the older boys tired of it and retreated next door to Percy's old tree house. The three older boys had no trouble clambering up the rope to the top and once there, let Chuck join them. Then they invited Jiff, who climbed the rope into the tree house.

But when Guy made to grab the rope and come up too, the older guys told him not to come.

"No little kids up here," called down Butch, which hurt Guy immensely seeing as how he was actually older than Jiff, and to be relegated with Mike and Don was out and out insulting.

"I'm almost a year older than Jiff," he protested, still holding the rope.

"So what?" said Jiff, laughing from somewhere inside the tree house. There was general giggling among the gathering up there then some low talk that Guy couldn't make out.

"Bet he's really younger than Mike!" said Butch.

"Yeah, he still plays with little army men," said Chuck.

By that point, Guy had released the rope and felt a lump rising in his throat. But he refused to cry. That would only prove that his tormentors were right about making fun of his age.

"Jiff, you comin' down?" he called up hopefully.

"No!"

Guy was too proud to keep asking, and turned to go. In his mind, Guy forgave Jiff. It was being around the big kids that made him forget himself. Made him forget that he and Guy were best friends. The only thing was to let him be for now. Later, when he went over to get him after supper, things would be back to normal. Instead, Guy went home, grabbed a book he'd been reading, and made his way to his own tree platform and settled down to be by himself. Alone with nothing but the blue sky overhead and camouflaged among the green leafage of the old maple tree, away from his problems, he was able to calm down and rest, contented.

It was some days later, when Guy and Jiff were back together, the events of the other day forgotten, that they were joined by Chuck who suggested a break in their routine.

"Wanna go see a kid I know down the street?" he asked, turning his head to spit.

"Who?" asked Jiff, interested.

"A kid from school. Name's Paul. He lives in the parsonage. His father's the pastor of the First Methodist."

"The white church that Jiff goes to?" asked Guy, spitting too.

"That's it," confirmed Chuck. "Wait'll you see his clubhouse! It's the coolest thing."

Immediately, both Jiff and Guy became interested.

"Really?" asked Jiff. "I wouldn't mind checking that out."

"Me too," agreed Guy.

"Then let's go."

Leading the way, Chuck took them through the Cardona's yard to the wooded space on the opposite side of the Therrien's from the field where they had played ball a few days before. There was a path leading into the woods there that Guy and Jiff and the others often used to play army among the trees and tall grass there.

"Where we goin'?" asked Guy, confused.

"Paul lives on the other side," said Chuck, pointing at a green colored house that poked up beyond the wood lot. Off to the right, the steeple of the white church rose farther up hill in the direction of Hovey Square.

In a few minutes, they emerged into the back yard of the parsonage that was flanked by a long shed supported by cinder blocks and a garage whose rear wall featured a basketball hoop.

"Doesn't seem to be anyone around," said Jiff.

Suddenly, a dog began to bark from inside the shed, having sensed their presence.

"Scared the daylights out of me!" said Guy, holding his chest in mock fright.

"That's Ranger, Paul's spaniel," explained Chuck. "Don't worry, he's friendly."

Just then, the rear door to the shed flung itself open and out tumbled a gaggle of kids, led by a red haired youth about their own age.

"Hey, Paul," greeted Chuck with a wave.

"Chuck!" said Paul. "What are you doin' here?"

Chuck shrugged. "Had nothin' to do and decided to show my friends here where you lived. Told 'em about your clubhouse."

"Chuck said it's really cool," said Jiff.

"Who're you?" Paul wanted to know. By this time, he and his friends had gathered around close.

"Jiff Jorgenson," replied Jiff.

"And I'm Guy DeMonde," added Guy.

"Friends of yours, Chuck?"

"Neighborhood friends," said Chuck. Then, turning to Jiff and Guy: "Paul's one of my school chums."

Guy nodded, knowing what he meant. He sometimes spent time with his own school friends whose relationship with him he kept separate from his neighborhood friends. It was a thing that sometimes happened.

"So. You want to see our clubhouse, huh?"

"Sure!"

"C'mon, then."

Paul led the way back to the shed, his friends falling in behind the newcomers.

When Guy stepped inside the shed, he wasn't immediately impressed. It was an ordinary storage area with a lawnmower, rakes, shovels and other gardening tools lying around. But Paul didn't stop, he continued on to a second, interior door that he pushed open, Ranger squeezing past his legs. Beyond, was a second room, one that fulfilled all of Guy's expectations of the perfect clubhouse!

There was a small table with mismatched chairs in the center of the room and a window in the back wall. A small book case held a number of Hardy Boys, Brains Benton, and Christopher Cool novels. But what most impressed both Guy and Jiff was what was displayed on the clubhouse walls: toy machine guns, pistols, and assorted other weapons of war.

"Wow!" Guy couldn't help exclaiming.

"Wicked cool!" agreed Jiff.

"Like it?" asked Paul, obviously pleased by the boys' reactions.

"You bet!"

"Wish we had something like this at home!"

"You haven't seen the best," said Paul, turning to one of his friends. "Sherm, show him your gun."

Sherm, who was taller than the rest, reached up to a replica of an M1 carbine that hung from pegs at the top of the display. Guy noticed that he took it down with some effort, as if it were heavy. Sherm held the gun in his hands and worked the bolt action lever.

"Want to hold it?" he asked Guy.

"Sure!"

Guy took the gun and almost dropped it!

"This thing weighs a ton," he declared, hefting it in his hands.

"That's because it's real," said Paul.

"Real? You're kiddin!"

"Nope. It actually belongs to Sherm's father. He brought it back from the war."

"No kiddin'! Boy, I wouldn't ever expect the real thing to be so heavy!"

"Part of the weight is due to the barrel being stuffed with wood," explained Sherm, pointing out the opening of the barrel. "No chance of using it for real that way."

"And your father let's you use it to play army?"

"Sure."

"Wow," sighed Guy, impressed all over again.

"Hey, we have a couple more guys back home," said Jiff. "Bet between us and you guys, we could have ourselves some good wars back in that woodlot."

"Bet we could," agreed Paul. The others nodded in agreement.

"Then we'll have to do that one of these days," said Jiff.

"No time today," said Chuck. "How 'bout throwin' some hoops?"

"OUTS or twenty-one?" asked one of the other kids.

The rest of their visit was taken up playing either game with Paul's basketball, games that were much better suited to Guy's attitude to sports: they presented little or no need for hurry up plays. Mostly just standing around and shooting for the hoop.

That soon changed after Chuck and Sherm argued over a shot and began to wrestle on the ground, urged on by the others. Jiff and Guy stood mostly silent, unused to such rough housing. For his part, Guy found it difficult to violate another person's personal space let alone fight with them. And when he did find himself the occasional target of schoolyard bullies, his response was usually a passive one as he waited for the aggressor to grow tired of someone who didn't fight back.

Just then, Chuck found himself hollering uncle and Sherm let him up.

Catching Jiff's eye, Chuck called him out. "Bet you couldn't do any better against him!"

Jiff shrugged.

"I'll take you on, Jiff," challenged Sherm, barely breathing hard.

Aware that he stood mostly among strangers and not willing to be seen as a coward, Jiff agreed to take on Sherm.

Somewhat nervously, Guy watched his friend circle around with Sherm before charging at him, throwing both of them to the ground. For a few minutes, the two flailed in the dirt with Jiff sometimes getting the upper hand and sometimes Sherm. Eventually, filthy and exhausted, both agreed to call the contest a draw.

"Guy, why don't you wrestle with Ronny," suggested Chuck. "He's about your size."

He and Ronny were in the same weight class but that didn't keep Guy from resenting Chuck's encouragement to keep the wrestling going, especially if it included him.

Why didn't he just keep his mouth shut, thought Guy. *Maybe everyone would've had enough.*

"I don't think Ronny's interested in wrestling me," said Guy aloud, hoping his guess was true.

"What about it, Ronny?" persisted Chuck. "You game?"

Ronny shrugged, suggesting that he was as enthusiastic for a match as Guy was. Which was to say, not at all.

Guy could see it in Ronny's body language, but as with himself, Guy knew that Ronny could no more turn down the challenge than he could. It would be interpreted as an act of cowardice, the same motivation that, Guy was sure, had forced Jiff into wrestling with Sherm.

"Okay, then," said Chuck. "Give 'em room!"

Reluctantly, Guy moved into the circle made by the other kids. He hated fighting. In the few encounters he'd had in the schoolyard, he always found it difficult to actually hit someone and in fact, never did. Now, however, he was forced into taking a more proactive role. At least with wrestling, there was no expectation of fisticuffs. It would just be a contest of strength.

While he was daydreaming, Ronny had charged him, catching him in the stomach. The force of the charge hurled them back with Guy hitting the ground first. Immediately, Ronny tried to pin his shoulders down for a quick victory but Guy's instincts took over and in trying to roll over, succeeded. He threw off Ronny and jumped on him in turn. Now was his chance to pin his opponent. He straddled him with a knee on either side of his waist and worked to grab his wrists in his hands. The others were shouting encouragement or yelling advice to their preferred contestant but Guy barely heard them as he concentrated on what he was trying to do.

Ronny, however, was not cooperating. He flailed his arms about trying to avoid Guy's hands while twisting his body to get out from under. But Guy had the advantage of leverage and stayed put until finally getting hold of Ronny's wrists and forcing his arms to the ground.

"One, two, three…" counted Chuck, as Ronny's friends urged him to greater effort.

Finally, Chuck finished the count and Guy was declared the winner.

Both boys scrambled to their feet, neither saying anything. Like Guy, maybe Ronny was slightly embarrassed. Not from losing but from having participated in the whole affair at all.

Chuck's pounding his back in congratulations and Jiff's words of admiration didn't do anything to soothe Guy's feelings. He couldn't exactly say what it was, but he felt no joy in victory, only a kind of guilt, of feeling ashamed of himself and pity for Ronny for having been dragged into the contest the same as he'd been.

"It must be near supper time," said Guy. "Why don't we head for home."

Sensing that their visit had reached a climax, Jiff agreed with his friend.

"Good idea, Guy," he said. "I'm tired anyway."

"Aw, c'mon, guys," pleaded Chuck. "We were just havin' fun! I'm ready for a rematch!"

"It's okay, Chuck," said Jiff. "You can stay if you want. But I'm with Guy. We're tired. See you guys some other time, okay?" he called to Paul and his friends. "We can play army."

"Any time, Jiff," said Paul. "See ya, Guy!"

Guy gave a tired wave. "See ya, guys."

Scuffed and scratched, with their clothes covered in ground in dirt and grass stains, Guy and Jiff headed back to the trail that led through the wood lot back to Desrosiers Street. Behind them, Chuck had quickly followed.

Tired and sore, Guy felt mostly resentment toward Chuck for getting the wrestling started. Before that, things had been going well between the two groups of kids, but once the wrestling began, play was turned into a question of honor and personal reputations. With those kinds of things at stake, friendly competition couldn't help but become more serious which in turn led to resentments. When they left, Guy could feel the tension between his friends and the others and he hated it. The thing was, he couldn't decide if he hated himself more for giving in to Chuck's challenge and not doing what he really wanted to do which was to refuse it. Why did it matter to him that the others might have thought he was afraid? That should only have mattered to him. Why couldn't he be himself and not what others wanted him to be?

He would have spit then, but something stopped him.

Instead, he swallowed the saliva and resisted the urge to expectorate. It'd be a struggle, but from that moment on, he was determined to quit the habit. He didn't know why it was suddenly so important to do so, but he was set on doing it...

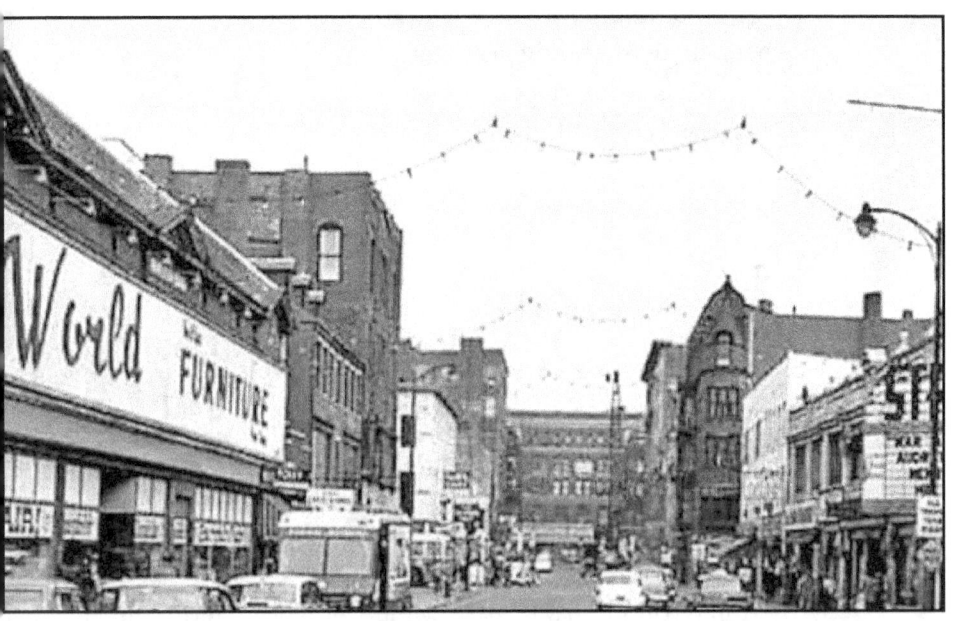

CHAPTER SIX

*In which Guy is betrayed
and takes a giant step back*

"Not graduating!"

"You heard me," said a disheartened Nick Tropoli.

"Just over that little fight?" asked Buster.

"Yeah. It wasn't so little as that."

Nick had been winning the fight that night at the graduation ball when it was interrupted by the commandant himself. The others got off with only a reprimand but he and the cadet he had been fighting, were reduced in grade and forced to re do their senior cadet year.

"This is awful!" declared Dan. "We were all going to be assigned to the *Attacker* together."

Nick shrugged in resignation. "You guys will have to go on by yourselves. Maybe I can be assigned to wherever you're serving next year."

"This is awful!" repeated Dan.

Buster remained silent.

Gateway to the Future
Guy DeMonde

"Keep quiet, you guys," said Jiff in an urgent whisper.

He, Guy, Chuck, Don, and Mike were approaching Tilden Street through the woods opposite Guy's house. They'd crossed Beaver Brook over a fallen tree then climbed the slope on the other side to a concrete wall built decades before after the Merrimack River had crested and flooded the neighborhoods on the other side.

"Why don't you guys wait here while I go ahead and scout the other side of the wall," whispered Guy. "I've been there before you know."

"Okay," agreed Jiff. "But remember your UNCLE training."

"Right!"

Carefully, Guy shouldered his way through a last stretch of tall grass, making sure to push it aside slowly so as not to cause a sound. At the same time, he watched his feet using bare patches of earth and rocks as stepping areas to further reduce noise. The gang considered their methods of soundless movement to be part of their UNCLE training as Jiff had said, or the way they imagined the super spies Napoleon Solo and Illya Kuryakin must have been trained in *The Man From UNCLE*, currently their favorite TV show.

The Man From UNCLE had debuted on NBC television the year before, but it had taken awhile for the boys' enthusiasm for it to translate into actual play. Mostly because they had no enemies to confront the way UNCLE had THRUSH. But when school began again the month before, and Guy was reintroduced to some of the kids from Tilden Street whom he sometimes hung around with, he was reminded how Bobby Toussaint had had a clubhouse in his backyard, the perfect target for a spying mission.

Not only that, but Bobby and his cousins, Deni and Normy Cardolet and hanger on Lester Beauchoin, could fit the bill as local THRUSH agents. Of course, that didn't necessarily mean that they'd think of themselves that way. In fact, they didn't, being bigger fans of the Hardy Boys books than the UNCLE TV show. Which later became a good enough reason for animosity between the two groups.

Reaching the wall, Guy slowly lifted his head until he could peek over the top.

They'd planned it just right. On the other side was the Toussaint's back yard, or rather, the field alongside their main house lot. The field itself was used by Bobby's father as a vegetable garden, just then looking forlorn with its dried up corn stalks standing in ragged rows. But alongside the wall, there was an uncultivated strip where a big apple tree filled the sky. It was at the base of the apple tree where Bobby's clubhouse was located.

Looking at it, Guy recalled the times he'd come over to Bobby's house and actually helped him work on the clubhouse. Bobby was never satisfied with it and was constantly taking it apart and rebuilding it until it reached its present form: a two story structure with a balcony on the second floor that let out onto one of the tree's larger branches. From there, wooden steps led to a crow's nest farther up. From up there, Guy knew, Desrosiers Street could be glimpsed across Beaver Brook.

The inside of the clubhouse was divided into a couple rooms downstairs, one of them an infirmary, and a single room upstairs equipped with bunks. Guy had to admit the whole thing was pretty impressive and wished UNCLE had such a set up. As it was, all they could do was hold their secret councils in his or Jiff's basements.

Not seeing anyone around, Guy was emboldened. He lifted his head higher for a better look around.

Across Tilden Street, where the Cardolets lived, there was no sign of THRUSH. Nor was there back at the Toussaint house. It looked all clear.

Turning, he signaled for the others to approach.

Impressed by how silently they all moved, Guy welcomed them to the wall.

"Doesn't look like there's anyone around," he whispered.

"Great," said Jiff, peeking over the wall for himself. "Let's you, me, and Chuck go over and search the clubhouse. Don, you and Mike stay here and keep a lookout."

The younger boys weren't happy about staying behind and missing out on the fun but they took their orders the way UNCLE agents should.

Quickly, the three others climbed onto the wall, their bellies hugging the rough concrete surface, before easing themselves down on the opposite side. Pausing only long enough to make sure everything was still quiet, they creeped over the shaggy grass to the corner of the clubhouse.

"So far, so good," said Jiff.

"Let's go inside," urged Chuck.

"Follow me," said Jiff.

The door leading inside was an old kitchen door Bobby had found someplace whose top half was open. Jiff poked his head inside to make sure no one was there and then told Chuck to stay outside and keep an eye out.

"Why me?"

"'Cause I'm in charge and Guy helped to build this place," said Jiff. "He knows his way around it."

"I still don't like it. No one's around. We should all be able to go inside."

"Can't take any chances," said Jiff, pushing open the bottom half of the door while trying to keep it from squeaking. After a cautious look around, he and Guy stepped inside.

Being there again reminded Guy of earlier days when he sometimes hung around with Bobby and other friends from St.

Louis Elementary School. It happened now and then but never lasted. He always ended up back with his neighborhood friends before too long. But this year, school had not even begun when he had one of the most profound shocks of his life: he found out that he would not be going on to fifth grade with Bobby and the others but staying back instead!

Guy had completed fourth grade the year before and had had no reason to think anything was amiss with his grades. They'd not been much different than previous years which was to say, average. Mostly C's with the occasional D in math. But none of that was a surprise. The surprise came just before his family's annual Labor Day trip to Canada when his parents lowered the boom.

"Huh?" was all a stunned Guy could say after hearing the bad news. "I'm staying back?"

"We found out a few weeks ago but didn't want to spoil your summer vacation by telling you too soon," explained his mother.

Although his father was strict about things like homework and grades, the fact that he himself had never graduated high school and had never been much of a reader, prevented him from mustering too much emotion about Guy staying back. However, what reaction he did give was devastating enough.

"When school starts," said his father, "I want you to get rid of your comic books. Throw them out. No more comics during the school year."

"No! Papa, not that!" begged Guy, already trying to imagine a life without regular doses of Spider-Man, Thor, or the Avengers. "Please! I promise to do better. I'll study more…"

But Mr. DeMonde only shook his head. "No. Your mother and I believe they're too much of a distraction. And no television on school nights either."

"But…my grades. They weren't any worse than usual."

"It wasn't just this year," said his mother. "It was the fact that you haven't improved them over the last couple of years. Too many Ds. Too many Cs. Your teachers believe that you can do better than that."

It was all just too unbelievable. Besides the humiliation of staying back, there was also the knowledge that now Jiff would be a grade ahead of him and he'd likely be sharing a class with his younger sisters. And worse, there would be no comic books for what might as well have been forever!

He brooded over the permutations of the news all through the family's Canada trip so that by the time he found himself walking to school on that first horrible morning, he felt like running back home and hiding under his bed. Not even the possession of a shiny new school bag with its brass clasp and cool subject dividers built inside could raise his spirits. Nor the new note pads and pencil case filled with unused pencils and erasers, water coloring kit for use on art days, and new Fireball XL-5 lunch box could do it.

Together with his sisters, he walked to school picking up other kids going the same way including friends they hadn't seen all summer. Guy wondered what they'd say if they knew he was staying back and blushed with embarrassment just thinking about it. At school, the school yard was already filled with milling children all abuzz about coming back for another year. Some were even running around or playing hopscotch already. *How could they feel so carefree and upbeat,* wondered Guy, *while I'm so miserable?*

Looking for a familiar face, Guy finally spotted Ricky Poilette over by the rectory garage and went over to him.

"Hey, Ricky," greeted Guy.

"Hey, yourself."

"What's the matter? Don't want to go back to school?"

Ricky seemed as depressed as Guy did.

"I'm stayin' back," was all Ricky said.

Guy immediately felt a slight rise in his mood. *I'm not alone!* he reassured himself, not without some feeling of guilt however. After all, he really didn't care to see his friend suffer the way he was.

"Stayin' back?" Was all Guy could muster. "You sure?"

"That's what my father said and he wasn't happy about it neither."

"I can imagine. Gee, Ricky. I'm sorry to hear that."

Ricky shrugged.

"If it's any help, I'm stayin' back too," he admitted.

Ricky immediately perked up. "You too?"

"Yeah."

"Well, I gotta admit, that's a relief. I thought I was the only dumb guy in our class."

"We're not dumb," insisted Guy. "We're both smart but in different ways than show up in our grades."

"Maybe. But in what way? If we get Ds or Fs we get Ds or Fs. What other way to find out is there?"

Guy didn't say anything but felt instinctively neither he nor Ricky was any dumber than anyone else. They just didn't study hard enough was all.

He was about to mention it when another voice intruded on them.

"I heard what you guys were sayin'" said Rocky Fourchin, joining them as he walked over from West Sixth Street. "You won't be alone. I'm stayin' back too."

"No kiddin'?" Guy and Ricky said at the same time. Rocky was known for playing a practical joke or two in his time.

Rocky shook his head. "No kiddin'."

"This makes it even more confusing," said Ricky. "We can't all be that bad!"

Something didn't add up, that was for sure, thought Guy. He knew for a fact that he, Ricky, and Rocky were just ordinary students, hardly any different than the other guys in the class. So why did the nuns pick on them to stay back? For sure, St. Louis had strict academic standards, more strict than the public schools. Still it was strange and inexplicable. The only reason Guy could come up with, and it was far fetched, was that the nuns must think that he and his friends were smarter than their grades indicated and that by keeping them back, they weren't punishing them but actually trying to help them!

This totally original thought was just beginning to sink in when it was interrupted by the ringing of a hand bell that echoed across the expansive school yard.

All activity stopped and slowly, hundreds of children began to gravitate toward an assembly area at the rear of the towering, red brick school building.

"Second graders, rooms A and B line up over here," said Seour Antoinette after the new first graders had already been led inside.

With the second graders in place, standing two by two with the girls in front, it was easy for the remaining grades from the third to the eighth to take their own places to the right of each other.

Guy and his friends were confused for a moment about where they should line up until Rocky shrugged and said "Might as well line up with the new fourth graders."

He wasn't sure about his friends, but Guy felt acutely embarrassed to have his former class mates including Bobby Toussaint, Don "Tornado" Nadeau, Geof Germain, and Mike Boucher, watch him line up with the new fourth graders in a public advertisement of his personal failure.

Of course, Guy had participated in this annual first day of school practice and had watched other kids stay back and join their new classes and recalled feeling embarrassed for them as well as relief that it hadn't been him. Well, now it was, and he now knew what those other unfortunate kids must have felt leaving their old classmates behind.

There was murmuring among the ranks at first as there always was, but soon enough everyone forgot about the students staying back as they concentrated on the new experiences and lessons they would have over the coming year.

Not so fortunate, Guy, like the other kids staying back, could only look forward to another year made boring by having to go over all the same lessons they covered the year before. *Phooey!*

Then, after each grade had been sorted out, the principal, a stern looking Seour Vincent, began her annual welcome back speech in a mix of French and English.

Having heard the speech before, Guy sort of tuned her out, as he felt a growing determination to bear down in the coming year to make sure he'd never stay back again. It'd happened before to some kids. Even a third time wasn't unknown. But when that happened, the kid usually disappeared from St. Louis to attend the local public school instead or even Santa Maria. The latter was located in a handsome stone mansion atop a hill along Lakeview Avenue. Again, operated by nuns, Guy had heard its classes were so small that it was almost as if students were being tutored. It may have been unfair, but students who ended up there were said to be "slow." Guy wanted to make sure that such a horrible fate never happened to him!

So, for Guy, it was bad enough to have stayed back, but worse was to come.

The first Saturday after that first week of school, his father told him to gather his comic book collection.

"What for?" asked Guy but he knew the answer: the dread day had arrived.

"I want you to get rid of them," said Mr. DeMonde. "No comic books while you're in school. From now on, after supper, it'll be only homework or reading. And if you don't want to do either one of those things, you can go to bed."

"Even on weekends?"

"You can do your homework on Saturday or Sunday, but no comic books at all. What's the matter?"

"I really didn't want to believe that you meant it before that you wanted me to get rid of my comics."

"It's your own fault. You should have done better in school."

Even though he'd been expecting the news ever since his parents had first told him that he was staying back, the demand still came as a devastating shock. How could he face a future without comic books? A whole year! Or at least most of a year clear to the following summer which might as well have been a whole year.

Still, the idea of simply throwing them in the trash was just too much for Guy to bear. Instead, he'd take them to a store downtown that friends at school told him about. A store that bought used books and old comic books. They paid two cents each for them and resold them at five cents so at least he'd be able to make some money from his personal disaster.

After asking Jiff if he wanted to go downtown with him, the two boys set off on their bikes.

"Do you know where this store is?" asked Jiff, as they set off on their trusty Schwinn's down busy Lakeview Avenue.

"Sorta," said Guy from over his shoulder. "The kids I talked to said it was on Central Street."

"Well, do ya know where Central Street is?" Jiff persisted.

"Not really, but I guess we can ask someone once we get downtown."

Guy had been downtown many times before but not by himself. Each week, his mother and a friend went shopping at the many stores there and lunched in the Dutch Tea Room. Each time, she'd take either his twin sisters or himself with her and it was an occasion they all looked forward to with eagerness because their mother would invariably buy them a little something before treating them to lunch at the Tea Room. Usually, going with his mother meant a book for Guy that he eagerly added to his meager collection of Tom Swift or Brains Benton sets.

But going downtown with his mother meant going by cab so that Guy only had a vague idea of how to get there let alone find his way around. He did know where Prince's book store was on Merrimack Street and figured to start there in the search for the used bookstore.

Riding their bikes on the sidewalks where possible, Guy and Jiff hugged the parked cars along the roads until reaching the city hall and veering onto Merrimack Street, the main drag in downtown Lowell. They passed the Bon Marche, the city's department store, and Pollard's, and Cherry and Webb before arriving at Prince's.

"Here it is," said Guy, pulling up in front of the store and leaning his bike gently against its plate glass display window. "Wait here. I'll go in and ask where the used book store is."

Inside, the store seemed narrow and crammed mostly with office supplies but it did have a modest display of new books ranged against one wall. Guy would have liked to look through them but hadn't the time. He waited for the proprietress to finish with a customer before asking about the used book store.

"A used book store?" wondered the woman. "Hmm. Let me see."

She went to a back room and Guy heard her talking to someone. When she came back, she had an answer.

"There's one right around the corner on Central Street," she said, gesturing vaguely in the direction of outside. "Go down about two blocks. It's called Harvey's."

"Thank you," said Guy and rejoined Jiff outside.

"It's around the corner," he told Jiff, remounting his bike.

"Is it far?"

"Don't think so."

They rode their bikes slowly along the sidewalk, careful to avoid the many pedestrians who crowded the midday streets. A street sign indicated Central Street and they cruised along, reading store signs as they went. Guy had just begun to wonder if he'd been given the wrong directions when they found it.

"Harvey's Bookland," read the unprofessional looking sign over the entrance of the store.

"This is it."

"Doesn't look very promising," said Jiff, cupping his face against the display window to see inside the darkened store. A few yellowing hard cover books lay just inside the window.

Leaning their bikes inside the foyer leading up to the door, they entered. A small bell over the door tinkled, signaling their arrival to the owner who was busy behind the counter pricing a stack of books.

"Hello, boys," he said in friendly greeting. "Looking for anything?"

Guy was still adjusting his eyes to the gloomy interior after coming in from the bright outdoors and so took a second to reply.

The only way he could tell he was in the right place was the musty scent of the store: the smell of pulp paper was heavy on the air. He lifted the bag he'd brought along with him.

"Do you buy old comic books?" he asked.

"Certainly do! Have you got any?"

In response, Guy made his way to the wooden counter and heaved up the heavy bag.

"My father wants me to get rid of them now that school's started," he explained.

"I know how that is," said the man, whom Guy assumed was the Harvey of the store's name. "Lots of kids come in about this time to do the same."

"Really?" In a funny way, knowing that he wasn't the only comic book reader to suffer the indignity of having to sell his collection made him feel a little better about it. But only a little.

Removing the comics from the bag, Harvey began to count them out.

"At two cents each, that comes to a dollar and sixty-four cents," he said. "Do you want that in cash or trade?"

"Huh?"

"Well, you can either take the dollar and sixty-four cents now, or you can pick out some books or more comics or records instead."

"Take the money," Jiff whispered in his ear.

"I'll take the cash," said Guy.

With a ring of the ancient cash register, Harvey reached in the drawer and counted out the money, handing it to Guy.

"There you go."

"Thank you."

Except on a birthday, Guy had never had so much money at one time and was a bit stunned by how much his comics had yielded. Too stunned to notice the rest of the store for a few moments. Not until Jiff called him over to some shelves that lined the wall opposite from the counter and on the other side of a rank of bins filled with old records.

"Guy, take a look at this!" said Jiff.

"What?"

But that was all Guy could get out before noticing what Jiff had been pointing too.

Shelf upon shelf of paperback books...and all science fiction! As Guy took a closer look, he was astonished to find all the authors he'd ever heard of from the free Scholastic Books catalogues the nuns handed out at school. Those catalogues always listed great sounding science fiction books that Guy never had the money to buy.

One by one, he went through the books on the dusty shelves, and looked longingly at their covers, some depicting astronauts adrift in space or exploring the surface of unknown worlds, some with streamlined rockets pulsing among the stars, some with alien monsters threatening beautiful maidens while others were less definite, with garishly painted covers that seemed intended to suggest weirdness rather than show it.

"These look great!" said Jiff, enthralled by the vistas opened up by the cover artists.

"I wanna read 'em all," said Guy, fingering the money Harvey had just given him. Idly, he wondered if his father would consider science fiction books as distracting as comic books and so forbid him to read them during the school year? Since his father had said that only home work or reading would be allowed after supper on school days, Guy reasoned that science fiction books would not be banned.

"I think I'll take a chance and buy one," he told Jiff.

"Can I borrow it to read when you're done?" asked Jiff.

"Sure."

With that incentive, Jiff helped Guy to pick a book that they both might like. Which wasn't hard since their tastes in the fantastic ran mostly in the same direction.

Unfortunately for Guy, however, none of the authors were familiar to him, making it hard to judge which books might be better than others. There was Isaac Asimov and Edmond Hamilton. Jack Williamson and Henry Kuttner. Philip K. Dick and John

Campbell. And there were whole shelves dedicated to Edgar Rice Burroughs whose name at that point, didn't mean anything to the boys. Finally, they decided on a book called *The Martian Chronicles* by Ray Bradbury.

"The stories all sound pretty good," noted Jiff as they perused the contents page.

"Yeah, and if they're all about Mars, how bad can it be?" agreed Guy, taking the book over to the counter.

"Find something, did you?" asked Harvey.

"You have a lot of cool science fiction books over there," said Guy, handing him twenty cents for the book (which, as it turned out, was a ridiculous bargain for a book that would transport the boys to incredible worlds of wonder)

"And I always have more coming in," said Harvey, slipping the book into a paper bag. "It's real popular."

Guy took the bag and the boys made their way back outdoors.

"Can't wait to read that book," said Jiff, backing his bike out onto the busy sidewalk.

"Me too. I just hope my father doesn't take it away from me."

"Why should he do that?"

"I don't know. My mother and father both think stuff like super-heroes and science fiction is crazy stuff."

"Huh. Well, if they do take it away, tell 'em to give it to me!" laughed Jiff.

Guy had to laugh along with his friend. The idea that his father would forbid the book did seem ridiculous. A book was a book. His father shouldn't have any objection to it...maybe.

"Hey, look over there," said Jiff, interrupting Guy's thoughts.

"Where?"

"Over there!"

Guy looked where Jiff was pointing and saw the marquee of a theater extending over the sidewalk across the street.

"The Strand," said Jiff, reading the name above the marquee.

"Didn't know there was a movie theater here."

"Me neither. Let's go over and take a look."

"Okay."

Waiting for a break in the steady flow of traffic along Central Street, the boys were able to cross when a traffic light down the street changed to red.

"C'mon!"

Together, they quickly walked their bikes across and reached the other side just as the light turned green.

"Over here," said Jiff, going over to some display cases to the side of the entrance which appeared to be a tunnel that led into the darkened interior of the theater.

In the cases, were framed stills from the movies being shown inside.

"Hey, look! The Beatles' new movie, *Help*."

Guy shrugged.

"*The Sound of Music*."

"My mother would probably like that," said Guy.

Together, they made their way along the wall before crossing to the other side and there, they hit paydirt.

"*Planet of the Vampires!*"

"Where?"

"Right here," exclaimed Jiff, pointing at a still showing an eerie scene from the movie.

"Aw, wicked!"

"I gotta see that one!"

"And look over here! *Die, Monster, Die!*"

"Is that Boris Karloff?"

"Yeah, says so here."

"Hey, does this say what I think it says?"

"What?"

"It's a double bill!"

"So?"

"Dummy! That means they're shown together, one after the other. For the price of one!"

"No kiddin'? That'd be a bargain all right."

"It says here on Saturday afternoon matinees it's only a dollar."

Suddenly, Guy balked. A dollar was real money.

"We gotta come back here and see these movies!" Jiff was saying.

It was easy for Jiff to say. His parents usually gave him money for things he wanted. But it'd be a lot harder for Guy to do the same. Especially after staying back. What's more, soon, his father would be quitting the ice cream route for the winter. That would put a severe cramp in his ability to earn money. If only he had that paper route! He felt the dollar bill he had in his pocket from selling his comics and considered. Was it worth it? He looked at the stills in the display case again: the spooky mansion and the zoo filled with monsters in *Die, Monster, Die* and the spaceships resting on the surface of a fog bound planet in *Planet of the Vampires* and his mind was made up.

"How 'bout next Saturday?"

"You're on!" said Jiff, ready to ride home with new found energy.

Together, they hopped aboard their bikes and headed back to the familiar Desrosiers Street neighborhood, the world having already begun to open up, revealing new and heretofore unsuspected possibilities.

Back at school the next Monday, Guy had finally settled in to the new routine, a routine that had become familiar to him due to having already covered the material the year before, including the same books. (Among which was The Founders of Freedom, covering Western Civilization and that contributed to Guy's mounting interest in the subject; in particular, he loved the book's maps describing the Roman, Holy Roman, and British Empires; history, as it turned out, had been his best subject) But he soon realized that the familiarity helped give him an advantage in his studies so that he was sure he could raise his grades with little more effort than usual.

Aside from his studies, he was able to reacquaint himself with school friends Ricky and Rocky. Added to the mix was Billy Beaulois, who developed a somewhat slavish attachment to Guy that could be annoying at times. Mostly when Guy decided to hang around with his neighborhood friends instead of his school friends. But Bill never got the message and insisted on following him home and inserting himself in their play.

Recently, Rocky's family had moved from a second floor apartment they'd rented near the school to a house on Lakeview Avenue. Soon after their move, Rocky invited the others over to have a look see. And though they were all happy to see that the Fourchins had moved into a big two story home, what really impressed them was what they found in the back yard.

"What about this shed?" asked Ricky.

"Right now, it's filled with junk the old owners left behind," replied Rocky. "But my Dad wants to get rid of it all as soon as he has the time."

"It would make a great clubhouse," observed Guy. "I know a kid who has almost the same kind of shed and he turned the back half into a clubhouse. It was really cool."

Rocky pushed the shed's rickety door inward with a scrape and stepped inside. The others followed but it was so crowded with junk, they could barely fit.

"See? With all this stuff in here, we can't even make it to the back," said Rocky.

Where they stood, the shed was piled high with cardboard boxes, old lawn equipment, and who knew what else. Over all was a thick smell of mustiness. There were mouse droppings on the floor.

"Wow," said Billy, his hands perpetually stuck in his pockets. "Gonna take a long time to empty this place out."

"Yeah," agreed Guy. "Reminds me that Bobby Toussaint has a clubhouse too. But he made his own from scratch; it wasn't a shed before or anything like that."

"I heard about it," said Rocky. "Wouldn't mind checking it out."

"I can show it to you one of these days," said Guy. "But it'll have to be on the sly 'cause me and my friends aren't exactly wanted over there."

"How come?" asked Rocky.

"Well we sorta started a war with them. UNCLE versus THRUSH. You know, like the TV show?"

"Really? I wouldn't mind bein' a part of that."

"Next time you come over, maybe you can join us," said Guy. UNCLE was always looking to recruit new agents! In fact, they hadn't made any new recruits beyond he, Jiff, Don, and Mike since they started while THRUSH had added a new kid, Lester Beauchoin, who'd moved into their neighborhood.

It was about a week later, as autumn was moving in quickly with trees beginning to blaze with colors of red, orange, and yellow and Halloween right around the corner, that Rocky came over one day after school.

Jiff was eager to introduce him to Jiff and the others but to his disappointment, none of them were around.

"Rats," said Guy, stepping down from Jiff's porch. "He stayed after school."

"Well, why don't you show me Bobby's clubhouse anyway?"

"Okay," agreed Guy, and led the way to Beaver Brook and the concrete wall that bordered Bobby's house.

"Wow, you were right," breathed Rocky as he gazed upon the two story splendor of the clubhouse. "And that crow's nest that leads out of the second floor is the coolest."

"I remember Bobby was always fooling around and rebuilding the clubhouse from the days when I used to hang around with him. He was always tearing parts of it down and improving it."

"Let's take a closer look," said Rocky.

"Okay," agreed Guy. "The coast looks clear."

Together, they slipped over the wall and dropped down on the other side, in the shadow of the apple tree whose leaves had fallen into a thick carpet beneath their feet.

"C'mon," said Guy, dashing for the door to the clubhouse.

Rocky was right behind him, eager to look inside.

"Slow down!" warned Guy as Rocky began to push the door in.

Luckily, there was no one inside and in another moment they were standing in the single ground floor room. There were items of furniture, cast offs looted from roadside trash pickups, a desk with pens and paper neatly placed, a row of Hardy Boys books on a shelf. A tiny room to the side, filling a small addition to the first floor was curtained off. Looking in, Guy saw that it was outfitted as an infirmary with boxes of band aids and rolls of gauze arranged neatly on shelves and a single bunk on the dirt floor. Likely it was where Bobby's sister acted as the gang's nurse.

"Will ya look at this," Guy was saying, but Rocky had already vanished up a ladder leading to the second floor. "For cryin' out loud!"

Going to the ladder, Guy called up in a loud whisper: "Rocky! Be careful! Bobby and Deni could still be around!"

Bobby's house was right on the other side of the field, and Deni, his cousin, directly across the street with the clubhouse in plain sight of both.

When Guy poked his head into the second floor space, he just had time to catch Rocky's legs as they disappeared onto a platform outside. Hoisting himself up, Guy found himself in a bunk room complete with home made matresses on the bunks and sleeping bags rolled up ready for use. Two actual glass windows gave views out to the field and Bobby's house. Quickly, he followed Rocky outside only to find he'd scrambled up the wooden steps to the upper reaches of the tree where the crow's nest was.

"This is so cool!" exclaimed Rocky. "I can see the whole neighborhood from up here."

"Get down from there," insisted Guy, getting more nervous by the moment. "They'll see you!"

"Okay, I'll...uh, oh."

A chill ran down Guy's spine. "What do you mean 'uh, oh?'"

"Somebody's comin' out of Deni's house," said Rocky. Then "It's Deni! And Bobby! And there's a couple of other guys with 'em!"

"Get down from there right now!" insisted Guy, panicking. "We've gotta get outta here before they get here!"

Not wanting to be trapped in the clubhouse when Bobby and Deni arrived, Guy dashed down the ladder without waiting for Rocky. Quickly, he went out the door and stopped. Bobby and Deni and yes, they had Lester and Normy with them too, were already across the street and at the garden gate.

"Rocky! Where are you?"

But there was no reply.

Bobby and Deni had separated, each taking one of the others with them in an obvious attempt to surround him.

"Rocky!" he called again. But time had run out. He'd have to run now or be captured!

He ran for the wall but it was higher on this side than it was on the other, making it harder to scramble up and over. The delay would be too long. Deni was already practically on top of him coming in from the right. Guy left the wall and dashed around to place the clubhouse between him and Deni.

Rounding the corner of the building, he almost ran into Normy but Normy was as surprised as he was allowing Guy to give him a good shove that landed him on his rear end amid the garden's dry stand of corn stalks. Without breaking his stride, Guy kept running. Just then, Lester leaped at him and while he was still about a foot off the ground, Guy did a most unusual thing for him. He punched Lester in the stomach, knocking the wind out of him!

By then, Bobby was on him, taking hold of his jacket. They struggled, swinging each other around and Guy wondered where the heck was Rocky? He'd still not appeared from inside the clubhouse. Was he afraid? Did he think he could hide in there? But Guy had no time to wonder any further, nor wait around for his friend. With a tear of fabric, he managed to break away from Bobby and run in the direction of Bobby's house. Tilden Street was a dead end but what Guy had heard from his father was that it was supposed to have hooked up with Desrosiers Street on the other side of the woods but was never completed. Running as fast as he could, he took a chance to look behind him and saw Bobby was hot on his trail. But ahead there was nothing. He was in the clear, so long as he could make the woods. He had no choice but to leave Rocky to his fate.

Which was where things stood when Guy had gathered the rest of the UNCLE agents for a rescue mission.

Luckily, Jiff's after school stay was not a serious issue and he was home when Guy arrived, still breathless from his narrow escape.

"Let's get the others, quick!" was all Jiff said after Guy had made his hurried explanations. "You find Mike and I'll get Don. We'll meet at Chuck's."

Guy found Mike raking leaves in his yard.

"C'mon! We got an UNCLE mission!"

Mike immediately dropped the rake he'd been using and ran after Guy, getting briefed on the mission on the way. By the time they'd gathered in front of Chuck's house, everyone was up to speed and they wasted no time making their way to the end of Desrosiers Street and entering the woods.

"So what's the deal with this Rocky guy?" asked Chuck. "Is he a jerk or what?"

"Of course not!" replied Guy, getting defensive about his friend. "He must have thought he was trapped in the clubhouse and couldn't risk coming out."

"Doesn't sound right to me," gruffed Chuck.

"All right, you guys," said Jiff. "Keep it down, we're almost at the wall."

"So, what's the plan?" asked Chuck. "We just goin' to bust in on 'em?"

"We'll see when we get there," said Jiff, who'd stuffed his new sling shot in his back pocket. It was very cool in that it had a built in sight in the handle to help with aiming. The others began to collect apples that had fallen to the ground on this side of the wall from the tree in the Toussaints' yard and stuffing their pockets with them.

Now, their pockets bulging with apples and more filling their hands, Jiff and Guy entered the quiet clubhouse. Inside, all was as Guy remembered it from the first time he was there with Rocky. There was no sign of a struggle.

Suddenly, there was a shout from outside and as they turned in the direction of the door, someone jumped down through the ladder hole leading to the second floor! It was Bobby Toussaint and right behind him came Rocky, hopping off the ladder two rungs short of the bottom.

"Rocky!" cried Guy, moving to maneuver Bobby into the far corner. "Out the door! Follow Jiff!"

But instead, Rocky moved to grab Guy in a bear hug!

"Rocky!" gasped Guy. "What're you doin'?"

"Some friend you got there, Guy," said Jiff, grabbing hold of Rocky's arms before Bobby could make a move. "Looks to me like he's a traitor!"

Guy ducked down and squeezed free of Rocky's embrace, then spun away toward the door. Jiff following.

"Are you a traitor?" asked Guy.

"Whatever you wanna call it," admitted Rocky.

"How come? I thought you wanted to join UNCLE?"

Rocky laughed. "That's corny. And besides, these guys have this cool clubhouse. Lots better than just meeting in someone's basement!"

In some part of his mind, Guy couldn't blame Rocky entirely for his about face. Bobby did have a great clubhouse, the kind he and his friends wished they had. But they comforted themselves in the knowledge that as UNCLE agents, they were in the right.

The next thing, Guy was outside the clubhouse with Jiff where Chuck was in a shoving match with Deni while Normy and Lester were kept busy by a constant barrage of apples being thrown by Don and Mike from behind the concrete wall.

"We gotta get out outta here," shouted Jiff. "We're outnumbered with your pal on their side and Don and Mike stuck on the other side of the wall."

"We need to make a run for it towards the woods," said Guy, recalling his successful escape by that route earlier in the day. By that point, the sun had begun to set behind the distant trees and shadows were lengthening across Bobby's yard. "C'mon, Chuck, head for the woods!"

Together, the three friends high tailed it for the end of the street, figuring that Don and Mike would see them and get the message to retreat themselves in the other direction. They'd meet again on Desrosiers Street.

Behind them, the entire THRUSH gang was hot on their heels but they reached the woods first and ducked into the brush, browning leaves crunching underfoot. Around them, most of the trees were stripped bare, their grey trunks seeming to meld together in a spooky, lonely feeling with only the occasional beam of fading sunlight among them.

"Faster!" said Jiff, leading the way, branches and thorn bushes brushing against his legs.

"They're right behind us," said Guy, bringing up the rear.

Gradually, by the sounds, it appeared that THRUSH had fallen behind but were still in pursuit. Still, the boys were able to burst out onto Desrosiers Street in plenty of time to reach Guy's yard and prepare to meet them. Jiff grabbed the slingshot from his back pocket and loaded it with a pebble he'd picked up. Then, just as Bobby emerged from the woods, he let fly a warning shot that whizzed overhead, slashing through some pine branches.

Bobby heard the sound and recognized it. He stopped, the others bunching up behind him.

"Don't come any closer or the next shot won't be a warning," called Jiff, pulling back on the rubber band of his slingshot.

Just then, Don and Mike ran over to join them.

"Slingshot, huh?" mocked Bobby. "We can play that game too!"

Turning to Deni, he motioned with his hand.

Deni produced his own slingshot. He kept pebbles in his pockets for just such an emergency. He loaded and let one go.

In Guy's yard, the boys ducked instinctively, hearing the pock sound as the flying pebble struck the side of the house.

Immediately, Lester followed up by throwing a rotten tomato in Don's direction. It fell short, but had the effect of starting a duel between he and Normy and Don and Mike as they threw the remainder of the apples they'd collected at each other. No hits were scored.

Meanwhile, Jiff had reloaded his slingshot and sent a pebble of his own toward Deni but made sure it stayed well above his head. In reality, neither side wanted things to escalate to the point where real injury might occur so he and Deni traded a few more desultory shots before everyone realized the battle had become a standoff.

After a while, Bobby and the others began to melt away into the woods, Rocky with them leaving Guy feeling frustrated and betrayed. He thought Rocky was his friend. And in fact, they were real tight at school and would remain so, both compartmentalizing their experiences here and not allowing it to interfere with their friendship away from Tilden Street. It would be a strange sort of truce and one neither would ever need to mention again despite Rocky joining THRUSH for one more encounter. A circumstance that relieved Guy not only for the preservation of a friendship he valued, but for his standing among his Desrosiers Street friends who might have suspected his judgment when it came to the friends he brought home from school.

"Well, I guess things didn't turn out so bad after all," said Jiff.

"I hope Guy'll pick better friends in the future," said Chuck.

"Ah, shuddup, Chuck," said Guy, defensively. "Anyone could make a mistake. It was Bobby's clubhouse that did it. Every time we get a new recruit for UNCLE, they get one look at that clubhouse and we lose 'em."

It was true. Such betrayals had happened before.

"Guy's right. Not his fault," agreed Don.

"Anyway, it was a great fight!" enthused Mike, an apple in each hand. "You see the way me and Don kept Lester at bay from over the wall?"

"And how Jiff scared 'em off with his slingshot?" said Chuck. "Lemme see that thing, Jiff."

As it was getting late, the boys broke up and went their separate ways. For Guy, it was almost supper time and then homework and studying to make sure he never stayed back at school again.

But thinking it over, he found himself secretly grateful for Rocky. His actions still ended up providing UNCLE with one its most thrilling battles yet. What a blast!

CHAPTER SEVEN

*In which Guy learns
that winning is not everything*

"Commandant's Office," read the shiny plaque on the door.

Nick Tropoli, newly graduated at last from the Inter Planet Space Force academy after repeating his senior year, stood nervously before the door as if it were the portal to Hades.

What did I do this time? He wondered for the hundredth time since receiving the order to report to the Commandant's Office. Mentally, he reviewed his recent actions: no fights that he recalled; his grades had been tops all year; no demerits; no reprimands. So what was it?

He repressed his trepidation and went inside. There, he was expected, and was ushered into the presence of the Commandant by his secretary. He stood at attention.

"Second Lieutenant Nicholas Tropoli reporting, sir!"

"At ease, lieutenant," said the Commandant, who was a big man, grizzled with long service in the astro lanes. "Lieutenant, I've been going over your transcripts here and must tell you how impressed I am."

Inside, Nick felt a little better.

"I thought keeping you back a year after that fight might have been a little harsh at the time, but I see now it did you a world of good," observed the Commandant. "Your grades have been exemplary this past year and for that reason, I'm promoting you to captain and giving you your first assignment as executive officer aboard the *Attacker*."

Nick was stunned!

Gateway to the Future
Guy DeMonde

"I hope Papa doesn't come home before the show is over," said Trece where she sat before the TV together with Guy and Marie. They were watching an exciting episode of *Lost in Space* where the Robinson family had just survived a raging whirlpool.

"Me too," agreed Marie.

"Don't say such a thing," warned Guy. "You might jinx us."

But it was too late.

Just then, their father's ice cream truck pulled up noisily in front of the house, its exterior lights so bright they lit up the whole street.

"Oh, no!" cried Trece.

"And only five minutes left!" moaned Marie.

"Maybe he'll get some customers to slow him down," hoped Guy, peeking out the window to check.

It didn't matter though. Mrs. DeMonde had snapped off the television, fearful that her husband would see the screen from outside. "Never mind that. Hurry up and get to your homework."

"Rats!" said Guy, getting to his feet.

"We never get to watch any of the shows our friends watch," complained Trece.

"Most of 'em are on too late anyway," noted Guy, thinking of *The Man From UNCLE* which was broadcast at 10 p.m. At least his new favorite, *The Wild, Wild West* was on earlier in the evening.

By then it was late October and Halloween just a week or so away. And though Guy and his friends looked forward eagerly to the holiday, it was okay if it didn't come too soon. That was because Guy's father would continue to run his ice cream truck till that date, giving Guy and his sisters one more week to sneak watching *Lost in Space* which had fulfilled all of Guy's expectations for science fiction after first seeing it previewed in *TV Guide* magazine.

He and Jiff had continued to follow their late summer ritual of buying themselves a copy of the magazine that previewed the fall lineups of the three main television stations. Every year, they eagerly looked forward to finding out what new science fiction and adventure shows would be premiering in the fall and this year had been particularly fruitful. There were of course, returning favorites such as *Voyage to the Bottom of the Sea, Branded, The Avengers*, and of course, *The Man From UNCLE* but among the new shows were also *Batman* (on twice a week!), *Lost in Space* (which the boys as budding science fiction fans following their discovery of Harvey's and the Strand, were especially hopeful for), and *The Wild, Wild West* that became a new favorite, up there with *The Man From UNCLE*.

Of course, some of the shows were broadcast beyond Guy's bedtime and so were missed (to his extreme frustration) or were shown on school nights where Mr. DeMonde's rule of "homework, read, or bed" applied. In those cases, Guy would be forced to listen to other kids' comments on the series until the following summer when he might catch them in reruns.

There was also the prospect of conflict of interest in that some of Guy's favorite shows were broadcast at the same time as other family favorites such as *Gidget, Bewitched, My Three Sons*, and *Disney's Wonderful World of Color*. Most of the time, he was outvoted by his siblings and of course, the overriding preferences of his parents. Luckily though, he still enjoyed the westerns his father watched and the sitcoms his mother and siblings liked.

But in the weeks just after school started, when his father was still at work early in the evenings, Guy and his sisters could count on his mother's more tender mercies to let them cheat a little on their father's strict after dinner rule to let them watch a favorite TV show...at least until the Mr. Softee truck trundled to a stop in front of the house. At which point, the TV would be hurriedly turned off and everyone scrambled to the kitchen table where their school books lay ready. When Mr. DeMonde arrived at the door with his money tray ready for his wife to count, he saw only three children hard at work with their school books.

"That was a close one," said Guy, looking up from the map he was drawing for geography class.

"I wish we could just watch shows like our friends do," said Marie.

"Me too. But it's not gonna happen. You know how stubborn Pa gets."

The others didn't reply, their silence was all Guy needed to know they agreed with him.

Still, Guy couldn't help feeling somewhat guilty at the subterfuge in watching TV behind his father's back. But sometimes, a situation was so dire, that you just had to bend the rules some time. Another one of those emergencies concerned his father's order that he not read comic books during the school year. As he'd feared, being able to abstain completely turned out to be impossible. The lure of the colorful adventures of the X-Men and Fantastic Four was just too much to resist. And so, Guy had disobeyed his father and kept buying the latest comics. He'd read them in secret in the basement and then hide them above the cardboard panels his mother had nailed to the rafters to cover up the wooden beams. When summer returned, his plan was to retrieve them with his father not being the wiser. Again, it was not an activity he was proud of and knew he'd have to bring it up in Confession the next time his class at school was brought to church for the purpose.

His religious obligations at church had loomed large lately and was the chief reason for Guy's guilty conscience.

"Quiet now, children, quiet," said Soeur Bernadette earlier that month, rapping her desk with a pointer. "Calm down. There will be a slight delay to the start of class this morning because Pere Andre has an announcement to make."

Immediately, the sudden quiet was broken by the murmur of voices among the students as they turned to each other with questioning looks.

"What's up?" whispered Ricky to Guy.

Guy shrugged. "Dunno."

"I know what's goin' on," said Rocky from his place behind Guy. "I got it from Jean Glaude in the other class."

"So, you gonna tell us or not?" asked Ricky.

"Pere Andre showed up yesterday morning in the other class to ask if anyone wanted to join the altar boys," said Rocky.

"Really?" Guy had never really thought about how or when the parish recruited its altar boys. In fact, he never even thought about becoming one himself. But now that Rocky had raised the subject, he suddenly found himself interested.

Just then, Pere Andre, his black cassock nearly sweeping the floor, stepped into the class and everyone stood up by their desks in respect.

"*Bonjour mon Pere*," said the students in singsong unison.

"*Bon jour, mes enfants*," replied Pere Andre. "Please take your seats."

And as everyone resumed their places, the young priest began to speak.

"As some of you know, every year the parish loses its older altar boys to high school. Of course, going to high school doesn't necessarily mean they have to leave, but some do. That means the parish finds itself short handed and the boys that remain have to pull extra duty so to speak. At least until we can find replacements for the boys who left. That's where you come in. You boys of course!"

Guy found himself interested, and in his mind, already could see himself in black cassock and white surplice serving at the altar during Mass, his family and friends in the congregation admiring him as he moved about and assisting the priest at communion.

"...so, if any boy here is interested, we'll be having our first welcome and orientation meeting in the basement of the rectory right after school today," Pere Andre was saying. Because of his daydreaming, Guy had missed most of the priest's speech but it didn't matter. He knew he'd be there at the rectory for the first meeting.

"You goin'?" whispered Ricky to Guy.

"Yeah. You?"

"Well, I'll go if you go," said Ricky, seeking reassurance that he wouldn't be the only one going.

"I'll go. What about you, Rocky?"

Rocky shrugged. "Might as well see how it goes."

Guy was happy that his friends would be joining him at the meeting and looked forward to being an altar boy with them.

"You think anyone else is goin?" asked Ricky, surveying the rest of the class.

"Deni for sure," said Guy, nodding in Deni's direction.

"You're right. What about Davey or Ron?"

"Could be."

"Hey, what about Billy?"

Guy craned his neck to catch sight of Billy sitting at the front of the class.

"Dunno. He doesn't seem very interested."

"Bill doesn't like doing anything he doesn't have to, especially homework," observed Ricky. "Not likely he's gonna like having to memorize the special prayers altar boys have to know."

"Probably." Guy didn't like that idea either but still wanted to at least give being an altar boy a try.

The rest of the day dragged on longer than usual as Guy eagerly awaited the hour when altar boy candidates were scheduled to gather in the rectory basement. Finally, the time arrived when the buzzer announcing the end of the school day sounded through the building and instead of heeding the call for "West Sixth right" to head for home, Guy accompanied his friends across the school yard to the rectory.

There, they saw a sign outside the basement door directing applicants inside.

Guy had never been in the rectory basement before. For that matter, he'd never been in the rectory at all so it was with a sense of adventure that he climbed down the steps into the basement and followed some boys ahead of him down a darkened passage to a large meeting room at the back. Inside, he was surprised to find almost every boy from both fourth grade classes beginning to fill up the folding chairs that lined the four walls of the room. A big table stood in the center and banks of fluorescent lights gave a sickly tinge to the proceedings.

Guy, together with Ricky and Rocky, took seats to one side of the room and waited for everyone to quiet down. Pere Andre directed traffic at first and when everyone was settled, began to speak.

"I'm really glad to see so many of you interested in serving God and your parish as altar boys," he said, looking around the room with pleasure and a beaming smile. "I'm not promising that it will be easy so I don't expect every last one of you to still be here even by next week, let alone after we begin your training. But I can promise that for those who stay, you'll have a most fulfilling experience and the satisfaction of pleasing God."

Guy hadn't thought about it in such lofty terms, but once the priest had brought it up, he couldn't help but seeing what he meant. Unconsciously, he sat up a little straighter and began to pay closer attention to everything Pere Andre said. By the time the first meeting was over, he was looking forward to the next when the official training would begin.

"You sticking with it?" asked Ricky.

"Sure," said Guy.

"Even after he warned us about having to know all the prayers in three languages?" said Rocky skeptically.

"Gotta admit, that didn't sound so easy but he did say we wouldn't have to memorize 'em. They got 'em printed on cards we can read from."

"Yeah, but Latin?"

"French and English I can handle," said Ricky. "The Latin might be tricky."

Guy shrugged. "I don't know. As long as we can just read it off the cards, how hard can it be?"

"I don't know..." said Rocky, shaking his head.

By the next meeting, a week later, Rocky had dropped out.

"Saw that comin'," whispered Ricky.

They were sitting together with about ten other boys in the front pew at church. More than half of the boys who'd shown up for that first meeting in the rectory had also dropped out leaving only the most dedicated which included not only Guy and Ricky, but Deni Cardolet as well.

Again, it was Pere Andre who spoke to them as he paced back and forth in front of the pew. Being the youngest of St. Louis Parish's three priests, training of new altar boys devolved upon him.

"Some of you are probably worried that being an altar boy will be too much for you, too much to remember," Pere Andre was saying. "Not true. But altar boys don't just stand around looking holy..." there were scattered giggles among the boys, "...they have things to do throughout the Mass...and before and after too. For instance."

Turning, he took up a two way candle lighter from a bench and held it up.

"I suppose you all know what this is for?"

"To light the candles on the altar," said someone.

"Right."

"And to snuff out the candles when Mass is over," said another.

"Also right. Which will be your first job when serving Mass. Depending on whether it's a high Mass or low Mass, you'll need to come out before the service to light the candles with this and then reverse it after Mass to put the candles out."

With that, he demonstrated with a sample candle.

"That's gonna be fun to do," whispered Ricky.

"Yeah," agreed Guy.

"There will be two altar boys serving at each Mass," continued Pere Andre. "And while one lights the candles, the other brings out the wine and water as well as the hand cloth and places them to the side, here."

So far, Guy heard nothing he wasn't already familiar with having seen altar boys serve Mass every Sunday since he made his First Communion in second grade.

From there, Pere Andre walked through the entire Mass indicating where and when altar boys needed to step in to perform their unique functions including ringing the hand bell during the Offertory, bringing the wine and water up to the altar for the officiating priest, "cleaning up" after communion by covering the cup with the chalice veil, and of course, reading responses and prayers off the cards placed at strategic spots at the proper times during the Mass.

By the time that second meeting was over, Pere Andre had begun to run the boys through the different portions of the Mass they needed to be familiar with in their roles as altar boys. By the time Guy emerged into the late afternoon sun, any remaining doubts he might have had about being able to be an altar boy had vanished.

"Whaddaya think?" asked Ricky as they crossed the school yard.

"I think it's gonna be fun," said Guy, confident that he could do it.

"I hope we get to serve together," said Ricky.

"Me too," said Guy. "That'd be cool!"

"Jean Glaude was tellin' me that if you serve funerals, they give you tips!"

"No kiddin'? How does he know that?"

"His big brother was an altar boy and he told 'em."

"I hope I get funerals to do then. I could use the money!"

But deep down, Guy knew money was no motivating factor at all in his desire to be an altar boy. It was something else. Something he could barely define. A sense of personal satisfaction and achievement, sure. But there was something more. Something more profound. It would be years before he could identify it but when he was able to, he realized it was a sense of feeling closer to God. Not just as an abstract figure seated on a throne in Heaven, but of a personal friend. A friend who would always be faithful. Who would never let him down, or make fun of him. Who would support him in all his interests and keep him company when he felt all alone.

In short, Guy felt good about being an altar boy!

As it did every year, Christmas rolled around, kicked into high gear as soon as Thanksgiving was over. Now it became even more important to accompany his mother on her weekly shopping trips downtown. Of course, she wasn't likely to buy anything for him while he was with her. She'd do that when it was his sisters' turn to go downtown. Guy's mission was to point out toys he wanted for Christmas to make sure his mother knew what to get him when he wasn't around. Sometimes the stratagem worked and sometimes it didn't.

Christmas that year was also helped along by a timely snowfall that left almost a foot of powdery snow on the Desrosiers Street neighborhood and everywhere else in Lowell. Just in time, as a matter of fact, to add an extra day on the week off from school that had already been scheduled between Christmas and New Years. It began with the distant blast of Dracut's emergency siren signaling to students that there would be no school that day. Guy and his sisters, already up to get ready for school were beside themselves at the sound. Almost always, the Dracut siren meant no school in Lowell too. And sure enough, when Mr. Demonde had turned on the TV to hear the morning news, there it was in a special crawl at the bottom of the screen: the list of towns and cities where school was canceled and Lowell was among them!

"Yippee!" cried Guy, dashing back to his room not to go back to bed, but to get dressed in his warmest clothing, ready for a full day's play outdoors in the swiftly gathering snow.

First, however, he had to help his father shovel out the walks around the house, the driveway, and around the fire hydrant in the front yard. By the time that was done, the same work had been completed at his friends' homes and he, Jiff, Mike, Don, Chuck, and the others were ready for fun and games. There was sledding down Dean Avenue, and building forts across the street from each other for snowball fights, and finally, the big kids had set up a long sledding course that ran down from Burnaby Street, through Don's yard, the Cardonas', across Desrosiers Street, and down into Jiff's driveway to his garage!

"Who wants to go first?" asked Chuck, breath steaming from his mouth.

"I will!" volunteered Don, throwing down his sled. He was about to get on when he was suddenly yanked back by the collar of his coat. "Hey!"

"Take it easy, half pint," said Butch. "We built this thing and we'll be the first to try it."

With great reluctance, Don stepped back as Butch threw his sled aside.

"Give me a good shove, Percy," said Butch after he'd taken Don's place at the start of the downhill course.

Percy stooped over and gave him a running start.

Everyone watched excitedly as Butch zoomed down the hill at top speed, barely able to stay on the course by steering his sled this way and that. At the street, Lewis watched for cars and signaled with his hands that it was clear. Without the need to slow down, Butch swished across Desrosiers Street and into the Jorgenson's driveway. He was going so fast, he had to bail out before he could crash into the garage!

Everyone at the top of the hill was jumping and clapping their hands with excitement and eagerness to have their turn at the course. Unfortunately for the younger kids, which by then also included Guy's sisters Trece and Marie, Polly Cardona, and Theo Agoulis, they had to contain their enthusiasm again as Percy took his place to run the course.

"C'mon, Sarah," he said, inviting Don's sister to join him on the way down.

Sarah lay on top of Percy's prone form as Jiff and Guy began to give them a shove.

Down they went at speed but before they could reach the street, a slight turn became a spill and the two older kids found themselves half buried in a snowbank.

"Wow!" exclaimed Mike. "I hope that happens to me! That looked like a blast!"

"My turn," said Chuck, shouldering aside Don and throwing his sled down. "Give me a shove."

"Aw, shove yourself," said Don, angry at being pushed aside.

"I'll do it," volunteered Jiff.

When Chuck had gone, Jiff took off, then Don, then Guy, followed by the others in turn. By the time they'd all gone down (not all making it to the street let alone the garage), the snow on the course had been reduced to a hard packed, even icy surface, that made sledding down go even faster. More often than not, people had to purposely bail out in order to avoid flying out of control or crashing into Jiff's garage.

It was such fun that it took the whole rest of the day, and after supper, the Therriens turned on their outside spotlights and the sledding went on well into the early evening. By the time Guy returned home, he was exhausted and his clothes soaked through. It was a great start for the Christmas vacation!

Still, the last few days before Christmas dragged until the big day finally arrived. Because the family would have to leave early for church the next day (where Guy would serve Mass) and then drive to Salem to spend Christmas day with their grandparents and cousins, they unwrapped their gifts on Christmas Eve. And though Guy would forget what everyone else got that year, he'd never forget the seven-in-one rifle his godmother gave him: it could launch smoke and explosive grenades, could fire plastic bullets, the trigger area could detach and become a hand pistol, and other functions. Perfect for playing war games with his friends. He also got a Monkey Division bazooka and a girders and panels construction set.

And the excitement of the holiday was far from over! More presents could be expected in Salem and playing all day with whatever toys his cousins received. After that, on the way home, they'd stop at their aunt's house in Lowell, where all of Mr. Demonde's family gathered for Christmas. There, with the family scattered among three floors of a tenement block, it was one huge party. And unlike his mother's side of the family in Salem, there would be a lot of smoking and drinking of alcohol, vices his own parents never indulged in.

Finally, after a long day, they'd arrive back home, Guy and his sisters and younger siblings all asleep in the car.

The next day, Guy went over to Jiff's house to see what he got for Christmas. Besides getting twice the amount of stuff Guy got (Jiff was the youngest of only three children after all while Guy had five siblings that his parents needed to buy gifts for), Jiff would often get the same things only more of it. And this year was no exception.

"Aw, neat! You got the Monkey Division Helmet, walkie talkies, and utility belt!"

"And with your bazooka, we'll be able to outfit a whole squad when we play army next summer," said Jiff, placing the helmet on his head and lowering the blue tinted visor over his eyes.

"Let's try the walkie talkies!"

"Okay. You stay here, and I'll go upstairs."

"Okay!"

Moments later, there was a crackle of static over Guy's walkie talkie set and he heard Jiff's voice coming over the speaker.

"...hear me?"

Guy pressed the send button and said "Just barely. Say again."

"Can you hear me?"

"Now I can! Perfect! This is so cool!"

"I heard that. Yeah, this is gonna be perfect the next time we fight THRUSH!"

"Oh, man. Yeah!" Guy was already imagining how useful the walkie talkies would be in their operations against the kids on Tilden Street.

Moments later, Jiff was back and they moved on to the girders and panels set he received. As Guy expected, it was the deluxe version, about twice the size of his own. It had everything including the pieces needed to build working draw bridges and elevators.

"I love this Fireball XL-5 you got," said Guy, holding up the scale model and admiring its detail.

"And it comes with the figures including the jet cycles that can fit inside the ship," said Jiff, demonstrating how it worked.

"This is great!"

"I also got a new football," said Jiff, tossing the ball up and down in his hands.

The rest of Christmas vacation was occupied by more sledding and snowball fights (including one with THRUSH) and being indoors playing with Jiff's new toys while in their stocking feet. Outside, more snow fell during the week and days were mostly overcast and gloomy.

But all good things eventually come to an end and after New Years, everyone was back in school. But for Guy and his school mates, there was one positive thing about being back in class, and that was the huge mountains of snow piled up after the plows had cleared the school yard of snow. In vain, the nuns tried to keep the boys off the mountains but it was no use. As soon as they turned their backs, the mountains were crawling with kids again, unable to resist playing king of the mountain with a hundred boys vying for the crown!

But now the short winter days began to lengthen and as spring approached again, the great mountains of snow began to shrink and melt away. By the time Easter came around, they were all gone and Guy had broken out his sneakers for the first time since Halloween. They felt so good on his feet! It was like a prison convict being set free from his ball and chain! He felt like he was going outside in his stocking feet! And then came the first day taking out his bike. At first it felt strange to be on it again and he had to find his balance again. But that didn't take long and soon he was dashing back and forth between his house and Jiff's, skidding to dusty stops in the dirt in front of his house and riding up to the library again where he made an amazing discovery: he found five more volumes to the Tarzan series by Edgar Rice Burroughs!

His interest in Tarzan had begun the year before when the family had made its annual visit to his uncle's farm in New Hampshire after his father had put away the ice cream truck for the season. There, he'd been poking around in the farm house's second floor store room when he noticed a box of books. By then, any collection of books was sure to attract his attention because he always hoped to find some science fiction books or at least some Tom Swift books. This time, there was nothing of much interest in the box except for one book called *Tarzan of the Apes*. Of course, he'd heard of Tarzan before. He and Jiff had watched a number of Tarzan movies on TV. But those had starred the actor Johnny Weismuller as a baby talking jungle man. So Guy wasn't too impressed finding a book about the character. However, in thumbing through the book, he noticed at the back there was an "ape/english dictionary!" What?! He'd never heard of such a thing but it immediately caught his interest. With some trepidation, he waited until just the right moment to bring up the subject with his aunt and finally asked her if he could have the book? She said yes and when he returned home, set about immediately to read it. It took him about two days to devour it. By the time he'd finished, he was not only a dyed in the wool Tarzan fan, but had acquired a whole new appreciation for the character. In the book, he wasn't any dumb "me Tarzan, you Jane" jungle man, but a self educated, well spoken hero who could be civilized and urbane one minute and a savage beast the next!

Guy thoroughly enjoyed the book which opened whole new vistas of imagination for him but he was saddened when he'd finished because there would be no more Tarzan adventures. Or so he thought. That spring day in the Dracut library he learned differently. There, he found additional volumes in the series including *The Return of Tarzan, The Son of Tarzan,* and *Tarzan and the Jewels of Opar* each representing incredible worlds of wonder and awe that fired Guy's imagination like never before. Well...at least not since he'd read the *Martian Chronicles* over the winter! The pleasure he took in reading had grown by leaps and bounds until he was never seen without a book in his hands. And when he didn't have a book to read, he became restless.

At first, he didn't know what it was. Like an itch he couldn't scratch. What was it that was bothering him? And what he soon realized was that it was the urge to create. It wasn't enough just to read stories written by others. He wanted, needed, to write his own stories. It was an awesome thought. Writing stories was something other people did, big time writers, not an ordinary kid like him. But the urge couldn't be denied. Ideas came to him while reading, or lying in bed at night or daydreaming in school. Ideas that he jotted down in a notebook. *Some day*, Guy thought, *I'll use them and write my own stories.* Carefully, hesitantly, in the weeks that followed, at night after his brothers were asleep, or alone in his tree platform, he began taking those ideas and turning them into little stories. At first only a few lines long, then a paragraph or two. Some day, he hoped, after he'd written a real story with a beginning and an end, he'd submit it to one of the science fiction magazines he'd seen at Prince's bookstore. And who knew? Maybe his name might be listed beside Ray Bradbury or Edgar Rice Burroughs? In the meantime, however, there was still plenty of excitement to keep a boy's life interesting. Excitement like the annual parish carnival that was due to open before school let out for the summer.

"Can't wait till this weekend!" said Billy.

"Me too," agreed Ricky.

"Which ride are you gonna go on first?" asked Rocky.

"The tilt-a-whirl," replied Guy.

"The tilt-a-whirl? Not me! I'm goin' on that ferris wheel," said Ricky. "Bet you can see the whole city from up there."

They all craned their necks and shaded their eyes against the glare of the sun as they studied the ferris wheel from where it towered at the deep back end of the parish's school yard.

The boys had been crowding the safety barriers that had been erected at the edge of the boys' section of the schoolyard to keep students away from where the annual parish carnival was being set up by a small army of roustabouts. They weren't alone. Scores of other students from all grades loitered at the barriers, watching with eagerness, the work of erecting the rides, game booths, and food stands that comprised the carnival.

"Boy, it sure didn't take 'em long to set it all up," noted Rocky.

"Yeah. They knocked together that ferris wheel in only a day. One day after school it wasn't there and the next, there it was," said Billy.

"Don't know if I trust going on it," said Guy. "Going up that fast, maybe somebody made a mistake some place. Forgot a screw or somethin' and the first ride, the whole thing'll come down."

"You think so?" asked Billy, suddenly wary.

"Get outta here!" said Rocky. "Those guys do this stuff all the time. They go from one parish to another. They don't make mistakes."

"How can you be so sure?"

"When's the last time you ever heard of a ferris wheel breaking down?"

No one could reply because no one had ever heard of such a thing. On the other hand, none of them paid much attention to the TV news or read the *Lowell Sun* either.

"Well, I'm not gonna let that spoil my fun," insisted Billy. "I'm still gonna go on the ferris wheel first."

Rocky shrugged. "Suit yourself."

"Guy. Your father gonna have his ice cream truck here like last year?" asked Ricky.

"Guess so."

Every year, Mr. DeMonde volunteered to leave his truck at the carnival all day Saturday and donate all he earned to the carnival fund. His soft ice cream would be added to the hot dogs and hamburgers, pizza, and fried chicken cooked up by other volunteers in the hopes of making a good haul for the parish.

The boys spent the rest of the noon recess watching the roustabouts hauling and banging and assembling the covered caterpiller ride even though none of them were interested in going on it when it was finished. It was deemed just a kiddie ride. Then the bell rang signaling the end of recess and it was back to class for the rest of the afternoon.

Time seemed to slow down over the rest of the week as Guy waited to go to the carnival that Saturday. The carnival opened on Thursday night but for the DeMonde family, school nights were out of the question. No way Guy and his siblings would be allowed to ignore their homework on weekday nights. But that was okay. It gave them more time to save money for Saturday, which was the last and biggest day of the carnival when most people would be attending.

And sure enough, that Saturday afternoon, as Guy, Jiff, and Chuck walked down Lakeview Avenue toward St. Louis Church and the carnival, the intervening neighborhoods were like a ghost town.

"Where is everybody?" asked Chuck, looking around at the empty, sun splashed streets.

"At the carnival, what else?" said Guy.

"Can't wait to go on those rides," said Jiff, who, as usual, had been given five dollars to spend by his parents while Guy was only given three.

"Not me," insisted Chuck. "I want that pizza! Only ten cents a slice!"

"Just so you can throw it up later after going on the whiplash? No thanks," said Jiff.

"Just don't go on the same ride as me after you eat," laughed Guy.

"Ah…!"

"Hey, Guy," asked Jiff. "What else are they gonna have?"

"Games like the hoop toss and target shooting and tossing darts at balloons."

"Anything else?"

"The bike contest," said Guy. "They're gonna raffle off new stingray bikes. One a boys' and the other a girls'"

"No foolin'?" said Chuck, newly interested. "With the banana seats and high handle bars?"

"Yeah. They had the bikes set up in the parish hall all week. The boys' bike is green, but not ordinary green. It's that green with the sparkles in it."

"Wow. I'd like to win that!"

"We can get tickets for the raffle when we get there. They're free."

"Then let's do that first thing," said Chuck.

As they drew into sight of St. Louis Church, more people began to appear on the sidewalks, all headed in the direction of the carnival with the ferris wheel poking above the rectory roof. It was already in operation, its seats filled with people, all pointing to views of the city unobservable from the ground.

Guy wondered if Billy was up there with them.

As the boys reached the school yard, the air was filled with noise, the combined sounds of kids screaming in mock fright from the various rides, the shouts of barkers at the various games of chance, music being pumped from speakers, and the general hubbub of hundreds of people as they laughed, talked, and shouted to one another to make themselves heard above the din.

From the rectory garage, came the smells of barbecue and fresh pizza.

Weaving their way among the crowds and lines waiting to get on rides, the boys made their way to the heart of the carnival where a central tent stood, its burlap sides rolled up to expose tables set up all on four sides and in the middle, a platform holding a pair of brand new stingray bikes, colorful streamers hanging from the ends of their handle bars.

"There they are!" said Chuck, pointing at the bikes.

"Let's get a closer look," said Jiff.

Guy said nothing, mesmerized by the sleek, racy lines of the green dappled stingray that he fervently hoped to win. He could just imagine himself riding it, dashing with ease over to Jiff's house or riding it downtown to the Strand with every other kid looking on with envy.

"Boy, there's a lot of people here," noted Chuck, as they began to squeeze their way past scores of other kids pressing against the tables and trying for a better look at the bikes. "Hope there's still some tickets left for us!"

Guy's heart leapt. What if they were too late? What if there *were* no tickets left? Suddenly, it became super important to reach those tables and Guy began pushing his way forward with renewed effort, bumping into another kid who'd turned away from the tables.

"Excuse me," Guy began to say until he recognized the other kid.

"No problem...hey! Guy! About time you showed up."

"Ricky! Are there any raffle tickets left?"

Because he lived right across the street from the school, Ricky had special permission to go home at noon to have lunch at home making him one of the most envied kids in school. The fact that it also enabled him to attend the carnival every night it was open before Saturday only added to his lustre.

"Plenty! Don't worry about that. But don't bother because I'm gonna win!"

"Why do you think that?"

Ricky showed him his blue ticket.

"See these numbers? Well the last two make thirteen. Lucky numbers."

"Maybe, but I'm not superstitious," replied Guy.

"Okay. You've been warned! See ya later." A moment later, Ricky had vanished among the crowd.

At last, Guy made it to one of the tables and saw that a number of ladies were working the pressing crowd of youngsters, tearing tickets off long rolls and handing them out while dropping their doubles into a rotating tumbler from which the matching ticket would be drawn later in the afternoon.

"Could I have a ticket for the boys' bike, please?" asked Guy of the first woman who came near him.

"Of course, young man," she said, tearing a blue ticket from a roll and handing it to Guy. "Now don't lose that. The drawing will be at four o'clock."

"Thank you," said Guy, turning away with a feeling of immense relief. He got there in time! There were tickets left! On the other hand, looking around him, he could already see what the odds would be for him to win the bike. Hundreds, maybe thousands, to one! His heart sank. He'd never be able to win. Especially considering that like Peter Parker in his Spider-Man comics, he never had any good luck.

"Did you get a ticket?" asked Jiff, suddenly appearing at his side.

"Yeah. You?"

Jiff held up his ticket for Guy to see.

"Now where's Chuck?"

"Right here," said Chuck coming at them from an unexpected direction.

"Where were you?" asked Jiff.

"Gettin' raffle tickets of course."

"Whaddaya mean 'tickets?' Like in more than one?"

Chuck nodded, holding up two tickets in his hand.

"How'd you do that?"

"Easy. With all these kids trying to get tickets, no way the ladies in there are gonna remember if somebody went up more than once. 'Specially if you go to another table and not to the same lady."

Jiff and Guy looked at each other.

"Go on," urged Chuck. "Try it."

"I don't know," said Guy. "That's like cheating."

"Ah, c'mon! Who's gonna know...or care? How likely is it that you're gonna win anyway?"

"What've we got to lose?" asked Jiff.

It was Guy's turn to shrug.

Together, they went around to the opposite side of the tent from where they picked up their first ticket and reaching the table there, discovered it was just as Chuck had said. It was a different lady giving out the tickets and she was so busy, she barely noticed them at all. The result was that both Jiff and Guy walked away with two tickets each.

"Any trouble?" asked Chuck when they met up with him again.

"Nope. Easy as pie," said Jiff.

"Well, we got a couple hours before the drawing, what ride do you want to hit first?"

After that, the time flew by as the boys tried every ride at the carnival...twice. They even went on the tilt-a-whirl three times! They tried the various gaming booths and as Guy began to bump into classmates from St. Louis, he drifted away from Jiff and Chuck. Sitting at a picnic table eating a generous slice of pizza, Guy wondered at seeing many of the girls in his class wandering through. Out of their school uniforms, in jeans and jumpers, they seemed completely different from the girls he saw every day in class. Watching them, he felt a tugging sensation deep inside until he realized that he was attracted by them. Having always dismissed girls as a nuisance, he found the novel sensation somehow disturbing but not unpleasant But before he could pursue the thought any further, Jiff and Chuck came up.

"So here you are," said Jiff.

"We've been looking all over for you," said Chuck, holding a box of popcorn.

"I figured if I stayed in one place long enough, you were bound to show up," replied Guy, tossing the crust of his pizza into a waste basket.

"It's almost time for the drawing," noted Jiff. "Let's go over to the main tent."

Just then, an announcement over the carnival's public address system reminded the crowds that the raffle was about to begin and most people began to drift in the direction of main tent.

Remaining on the outskirts of the crowd, the boys took out their tickets and held them so they could compare the numbers on them to whatever numbers were called out by the master of ceremonies.

"Think one of us will win?" asked Jiff.

"Hope so," said Chuck, "but don't count on it. Look at all these people! The chances of winning are pretty low."

Guy didn't say anything, secretly clinging to the hope that he might really win.

"Okay now, folks," the MC said, speaking into a microphone. He was standing on a milk crate that allowed everyone in the crowd to see him. To his rear, the two bikes gleamed in the late afternoon sunlight and it seemed to Guy that right at that moment, everyone held their collective breaths and all activity at the carnival came to a halt. All he could hear was the MC's voice as he continued. "Let's have some quiet now. As you know, we have two brand new bicycles here that some lucky boy and girl will soon be the proud owners of. I want to thank Hank Michaud of HM Hardware on Lakeview Avenue for donating the two bikes. Hank, are you out there somewhere?"

A man waved from somewhere up front but Guy couldn't see him due to the crowd.

"Here you go," said the MC, indicating the man who had waved. "Lets give a hand to Hank!"

Everyone clapped and cheered and some whistled for Mr. Michaud's generosity.

"That's wonderful, wonderful," said the MC. "Now boys only; have your blue tickets ready and if your number matches the one I read off...well, all I can say is, don't lose it!"

Everyone in the crowd laughed along with the man as he turned to one of the ticket ladies and said "Martha, why don't you start the gizmo?"

Dutifully, the woman began to crank a handle and the tumbler containing hundreds of tickets began to revolve, mixing the tickets thoroughly.

"I think that's enough," said the MC. "Why don't you dig deep and pick out the winning ticket?"

The woman did so and handed the ticket to the MC.

"Nine, four, zero, two, one," he read. "Anyone have that number? Don't be shy now. Nine, four, zero, two, one. Anyone?"

"Rats," said Guy, noting that the number matched neither of his tickets.

But his spirits rose when no one present spoke up.

"No one?" asked the MC. "Okay. Back to the tumbler."

The lady began cranking the tumbler again and stopped. She chose another ticket and handed it to the MC.

"Okay, let's try this number: Seven, three, zero, zero, three. That's seven, three, zero, zero, three."

Calmly, Guy scanned his two tickets and then it happened! He couldn't believe it! He must've been wrong! But it looked to him like he had the matching number! Then, the MC repeated the number again and to Guy's delight it continued to match one of his tickets.

"Anybody?" asked the MC.

"Here!" cried Guy excitedly. "Here! I have it!"

"Well c'mon up young man and we'll check your ticket."

A general murmur of voices sprung up all around him as the crowd registered both excitement and disappointment but Guy never heard any of it. He never even remembered if Jiff and Chuck had said anything to him as he moved quickly to the front of the crowd and the main tent. But when he was almost there, he thought he heard someone say that he had two tickets in his hand! The comment reminded him of his earlier doubts about taking two tickets but his desire for the new bike was so strong, he couldn't make himself turn back or admit that he'd cheated. Instead, he surreptitiously dropped the losing ticket among the milling throng so that by the time he arrived at the front and was lifted onto the table there, he had only the single winning ticket in his hand.

The MC took it and compared the number with the one that had been called and said "Looks like we have a winner!" The people cheered and clapped and Guy could see many of his classmates among them including some of the girls. For some reason, it seemed important to him that those girls see how he was the center of attention. But why?

"What's your name, son?" asked the MC.

"Guy," said Guy, still somewhat dazed as he looked out over the crowd. "Guy DeMonde."

"I do believe this is the son of our own Mr. Softee who is holding down his ice cream truck by the food court," said the MC. "Well, what do you think about winning such a beautiful new bicycle, Guy?"

"I think it's cool!" As soon as he said it, Guy felt like a fool. Every time he became the object of attention he became nervous and tongue tied. But luckily, no one seemed to notice or care as he was lowered back to the ground.

A couple men took the bike down from the platform and set it down next to Guy on the other side of the table. There, his picture was taken with Mr. Michaud shaking his hand.

"Go on, son," urged Mr. Michaud. "Try it on for size!"

No one had to ask Guy twice! Eagerly, Guy sat down behind the handlebars, feeling the comfort of the banana seat. Reaching for the high handlebars, he felt that they were at just the right height.

"What do you think?" asked Mr. Michaud.

"I think it's great!"

"Then let 'er fly!"

Guy walked the bike until he cleared the admiring crowd. Then, aiming toward the empty portion of the school yard, he stood on the pedals and began riding around on the hard tarmac. Picking up speed and with the wind whipping through his short cropped hair, it was everything he'd dreamed it would be. He felt free as a bird and the bike handled so smoothly! After taking two or three spins around the school yard, he finally came to stop in front of Jiff and Chuck. Ricky and Billy and some of his other school mates were there too, all watching him ride and all wanting a turn themselves.

Guy obliged and for the next hour or so, watched as his friends tried out his new bike. Watching others ride it, seeing it swoop and swerve, rather than riding it himself, he had a whole new appreciation for its utter coolness. And it was his!

After a while, when the thrill had worn off some and the others had drifted off back to the carnival (Guy never did find out who won the girls' bike), he and Jiff and Chuck decided to head back home. On the way, they stopped at Mr. DeMonde's truck for an ice cream.

"What was all the excitement about?" asked his father, handing him a chocolate cone. "You won the bike?"

"Yeah," said Guy, still astride the stingray. "Whaddaya think?"

"I think you better be careful it doesn't get stolen."

Guy had never thought of that! Such a cool bike, it would likely be the target of every punk kid in town. Would he, for instance, feel comfortable leaving it in the Strand's lobby while going inside to watch the movie? Or outside Harvey's while he browsed the books?

Quickly, he brushed aside the concern, determined not to let anything dampen his joy about beating the odds and finally winning something. His losing streak was over. He didn't care anymore that he stayed back or had to sell his comics. He'd won! Except there was something that still bothered him. Something that prevented him from freely embracing his good fortune.

He couldn't help thinking that he'd won the bike under false pretenses. He'd cheated in order to win. He'd had two tickets when everyone else had only one. It was a circumstance that would bother him long after the excitement of possessing the new stingray wore off.

CHAPTER EIGHT

In which Guy takes a wrong turn

"Ten hut!"

The command was uttered by Nick Tropoli as the ship's commander entered the control room of the *Attacker*. Immediately, the score of crew members gathered there, came to attention.

"At ease," said the commander as he took his place in the center of the room.

As the crew resumed their duties, Nick looked around to make sure everything was ship shape. As executive officer, he was second in charge of the ship and took his duties seriously.

The problem however, was that his friends, Dan and Buster, who also served on the *Attacker* but in inferior capacities, could not help but resent it. Nick could not help that but determined to make it up to them with the next shore leave.

For now though, he had responsibility and some independence as second in command and he did not intend to squander the opportunity!

Gateway to the Future
Guy DeMonde

Financially independent at last!

Guy didn't know where he'd heard the phrase before, probably on television, but it sure fit his new circumstances!

The event that lifted him from having to rely on the dollar he made every week (and only in the summers at that) washing his father's Mister Softee truck to cover all of his expenses, was getting a paper route!

It had happened late in the spring, just before school let out for summer vacation, when someone from the Lowell Sun had called Mr. DeMonde to let him know that a route had opened up in the neighborhood if his son was still interested.

"Are you?" Mr. DeMonde asked Guy.

"Sure I am," replied Guy and immediately began to consider the ramifications of accepting.

"Remember," said his father, proceeding to list the drawbacks, "you'll have to deliver your papers seven days a week. If you want to take time off, you'll have to find someone to take over for you. And Sunday papers are going to be big and fat. You've seen them. You won't be able to hold them all under your arm. You'll probably have to make several trips to deliver them all."

"I know," said Guy, not without some concern. But darn it! He needed the money a paper route would give him. Besides being able to start buying his comic books again, keeping up with the latest trading card sets, and the books that were becoming of increasing interest to him (not to mention candy and other sundries that were always tempting him at Hovey Square Variety), he had plans to begin buying accessories for his new bike (like a headlight and generator, rear signal flashers, and especially a lock and chain to help secure it when he went to places like the Strand downtown. "But I still want it."

Mr. DeMonde shrugged. "All right. I'll call the man in the distribution department and let him know."

That was three weeks ago.

Guy had since learned that his route would mostly cover the neighborhoods down the street through which he walked on the way to school so they weren't unknown to him. There were a few outlying customers back up Lakeview Avenue toward home but mostly they were concentrated in Centralville's "little downtown." There, among his customers, were Russell's clothing store (where his mother bought his school uniforms), the Cameo Diner (across the street from the tenement where his father's relatives lived), the Lowell Provision Company (local butcher shop), Blazon's Florist, Michaud Hardware, and the Centralville Social Club (a bar where he would sometimes see his uncle).

In addition, there were a few dozen residential customers up and down the side streets who lived mostly in tenement buildings requiring a lot of running up and down staircases. The worst was behind the Cameo Diner whose kitchen exhaust was pumped into the courtyard of a pair of tenements and that stunk so bad, Guy had to hold his breath the entire time he was running up and down the stairs. Elsewhere, he had to deal with a dog named...well...dog! At that house, he had to hope the vicious little creature was indoors when he delivered the paper. Otherwise, he had to find some way to decoy it away from the front the door giving himself time to run up and throw the paper on the top step and get off the property in a hurry.

But worst of all was a house located down a short private street leading to St. Louis Park. A kid lived there who took great pleasure in trying to pick fights with Guy. All Guy wanted to do was deliver the paper and get out of there, but if the kid was around, he wouldn't let him, often trying to get Guy into a head lock and refusing to let go. Guy, being essentially a harmless soul, didn't really know what to do. He was sure that if he fought back, it would only antagonize the kid more and numerous complaints to the kid's parents yielded promises to make the kid stop but without results.

By and large, Guy enjoyed his paper route and hated to lose even a single customer which would cut into his profits, but he was at the point that he felt he had to quit delivering the paper to that house.

Besides the punk kid, certainly there were times when Guy wondered why he'd ever taken on the paper route. It was difficult to deliver them day after day when he knew his friends were back home having fun. He had to go to the corner in front of Blazon's Florist to pick up his bundle of papers along with a couple of other kids, break down the bundle, and then using his bike, deliver the papers to different sections of his route before coming back to the corner to get more.

He had to do all that rain or shine and could only dread having to do it when winter came around again and he didn't have his bike to help get it done quicker. In fact, the route itself was responsible for his not having the money he'd expected to buy comics and books. The first few weeks' profits had to be spent on a lock and chain to secure the bike against theft and a pair of saddle baskets that he fastened over the rear wheel (cutting down considerably on the bike's cool factor) so that he could carry all of his papers with him and saving him time in going back and forth to the corner.

"So you're getting' tired of the paper route already?" asked Jiff one day.

"Did I say that?" asked Guy.

"You didn't have to," said Jiff. "You keep askin' if you missed anything while you were gone."

Guy shrugged. "Well, did I?"

They were sitting on the Jorgenson's front steps watching the girls at Polly's house across the street trying to walk on a pair of stilts Percy had made.

"Oh, sure, lots of stuff," said Chuck, laughing.

"C'mon, did I?"

"Just the usual stuff," said Don. "Mostly these guys don't wanna do anything so me and Mike have to play by ourselves."

"You get tired of playin' spongeball off your basement wall all the time, Don," said Jiff.

"Yeah, that's kid stuff," said Chuck, spitting.

"You play every time Butch and the other big kids ask you."

"That's different."

"Yeah, right."

Judging from the exchange among his friends, Guy guessed there was some rift growing among them. Don and Mike were two years younger than he, Jiff, and Chuck. Were their interests dividing? Already, he knew, that Jiff's interest in comic books had waned to the point where he no longer read them. Nor did he collect trading cards the way Guy did. They still shared an interest in science fiction both reading books and watching it on TV or at the Strand but how long would that last? It was something Guy had never considered until now.

"We play kick the can with you guys don't we?" asked Jiff.

"Sure but that's 'cause the girls are playing," returned Don. "If they didn't play, bet you wouldn't either."

"Would too."

"Would not."

They lapsed into silence then, neither having won the argument but Guy couldn't help thinking that there was something to what Don had said. He'd struck closer to the truth than anyone there would have cared to admit. As he'd noticed at the carnival, what girls thought or felt about him suddenly seemed to matter. He didn't understand what it was, but he knew (and would never admit) that playing kick the can after dark was more fun with girls like Polly and Theo (Guy didn't count his sisters) than without them. *Why should that be?* he wondered.

"So what do you think isn't kid stuff?" asked Don, breaking Guy's train of thought.

Chuck shrugged. "I know it isn't playin' sponge ball all day."

"Then what do you wanna do?"

"Wanna go and see what THRUSH is doin'?" asked Mike.

Chuck snorted. "That's kid stuff too. I don't even watch *The Man From UNCLE* any more."

The others gasped.

"I watch *Peyton Place* now," said Chuck.

Eyebrows were raised in surprise. *Peyton Place* was an adult show with a sordid reputation...at least in Guy's house it did.

"Yeah," continued Chuck with an air of superiority. "Me and my brother watch it. It's got plenty of good lookin' girls in it and plenty of kissin' and huggin'...pettin's what my father calls it."

"Yuch," said Mike.

"You really watch that show?" asked Guy, incredulous.

"Yeah. Why? Don't believe me?"

Guy remained silent. Knowing that it was perfectly possible after all that he'd learned of Chuck's family arrangements, including his parents' being divorced, which ran counter to every other family he knew of.

"That's boring," insisted Don. "Soap opera stuff."

"Don't knock it till ya try it," said Chuck philosophically.

Guy had been about to suggest playing little army men, but stopped, fearful that Jiff would join Chuck in calling it kid stuff. In truth, they hadn't played with Jiff's army set since last summer. Had he seen the last of those great battles they waged beneath the hedges and in the sand along the street?

"Well, I'm not gonna sit around here doin' nothin'," said Don, getting to his feet. "Wanna play sponge ball at my house, Mike?"

"Sure," said Mike. "You guys comin'?"

The others didn't rise. Guy would have but decided to stick with Jiff and Chuck instead.

"So if everything's kid stuff to you now, what isn't?" Jiff asked Chuck after the others had gone.

Chuck shrugged.

"What does your big brother do?" Jiff persisted.

"Hangs around with his friends," said Chuck. "He talks about girls a lot."

"Not much goin' on there," said Jiff, disappointed.

"He started to smoke cigarettes."

"Your father doesn't mind?" asked Guy. No way he could even imagine doing such a thing even though many of his father's relatives smoked.

"Nah."

"You gonna start smokin'?"

Chuck shrugged and spit. "Maybe."

"I tried a cigarette once," admitted Jiff. "Found it on the ground while it was still lit. Didn't like it."

"There are different kinds of cigarettes. Maybe that one was one that didn't suit you."

"Maybe, but I doubt it."

Chuck was silent then, thinking. Then he stood up.

"I'll catch up with you guys later," he said. "Nothin' doin' here anyway."

"See ya, Chuck," said Jiff with a little wave.

"Yeah. See ya," echoed Guy. Then turning to Jiff, asked "Waddaya wanna do now?"

It was Jiff's turn to shrug.

"Wanna ride bikes?"

"Nah."

"Go up to the library?"

"Nah."

"Wanna go pick raspberries? There were a lot of red ones on the bushes down at the brook."

Jiff perked up at that. "Yeah, okay. Lemme go in and get a bowl to put them in."

It was just on the cusp of summer and the early raspberries were turning red but not yet purple and the two boys were able to fill a good sized bowl with the berries.

"Remember how we used to come down here to catch hoppy toads?" said Guy, trying to kindle a nostalgic mood in his friend of early memories unshared by Chuck and the others.

"Yeah. Haven't seen many frogs around lately though."

"Wonder why that is? Some years they're all over the place and other times there's none around."

"Sewing needles too. Haven't seen one all spring."

"By the way, Jiff, is your cousin Morgan comin' up this year?"

"Dunno. Hope so. Or maybe they'll send me to Alabama instead."

"Hope not!" Being without his best friend for two weeks in the prime summer vacation time would be an eternity, thought Guy.

"You might not, but Alabama is fun. We hang out with Morgan's friends, go to the movies, take drives to places. And the weather is always fine. Never rains. And the last time I was there, I met a girl. Her name was Alice."

"You never told me about that!" *Girls again*, thought Guy. *We never used to give them the time of day!*

"Didn't think you'd be interested. I wasn't much...at the time," admitted Jiff.

"Waddaya mean, at the time?"

Jiff shrugged. "When I found out that I might be going to Alabama this year, I started to think about the last time I was there and remembered Alice. She was kinda cute. And she wasn't like the girls here. In the South, girls are more...I don't know...friendly? They don't mind hangin' out with the guys."

For some reason, Guy could understand how that might be exciting in a way but quickly pushed the thought away, embarrassed to even be thinking about such things. But unbidden, he recalled the thrill he'd felt when those girls had kissed him on his last vacation to Salem. Oh! It was all so confusing!

"C'mon," said Jiff, interrupting his thoughts. "We got plenty."

They returned to the Jorgenson's house, entering through the cellar door. It was dark inside with the few small cellar windows allowing only some dim light into the farther corners of the basement.

"Hey! What was that?" cried Guy.

"What was what?"

"I saw something flash in the bowl of raspberries!"

"C'mon!"

"No, really," said Guy, holding the bowl in his hands.

"There it is again! You see it?"

"Awww Yeaaaaah," said Jiff in his characteristic drawl.

"What is it?"

"Dunno."

The light came again from amidst the berries. The boys waited, holding their breaths. It happened again.

"Only one thing I can think of," said Jiff.

"What?"

"A lightning bug. We must've accidentally picked a lightning bug while we were picking the berries."

It was the nuttiest thing Guy had ever heard but he had to admit that no other explanation made sense.

Just then, the flash appeared a few feet away from the bowl.

"There it goes!"

The flash came again, a bit farther away.

"Quick, open the door," said Guy. "Maybe it'll fly out."

Jiff did that, suddenly lighting up the whole basement with the late afternoon sunlight. They caught one more glimpse of a flash and then there was nothing for a long time.

"Guess he must've found his way out," said Guy.

Jiff closed the door again. "That was weird!"

Later, after they'd split the raspberries, it was time for Guy to leave for his paper route. As usual now that school was winding down and the fine spring weather was drawing all the kids outdoors, he found himself reluctant to go to work. The feeling that he was missing out on the fun grew stronger the longer he was away from the neighborhood, compelling him to try and complete his route as quickly as possible. With the longer days, his father had begun to ease his homework rule and letting Guy and his sisters out to play until the streetlights came on in the early evening.

So the days passed until school finally let out for summer. The last day in school was only a half day with the morning given over to a final meeting with the class officers and then a farewell party the highlight of which was a comedy skit put on by Guy, Ricky, and Billy. Then, just before noon, students were released, shouting and laughing with joy knowing they had endless weeks (or so it seemed to them) of nothing to do but having fun!

But it wasn't to be all fun for Guy. Besides his paper route, he was still picking up extra money washing his father's ice cream truck which he did every Saturday morning and sometimes helped his sisters making the chilleroos. Still, there was plenty of time left over for hanging out with his friends, watching monster movies on TV with Jiff, riding their bikes to the Strand on Saturday afternoons, going to the Dracut Library, going up to the Van der Sands to go swimming, playing kick the can, and keeping up with the latest comic books.

Then, one day, Chuck said he had a surprise for them.

"What is it?" asked Jiff.

"If I told you, it wouldn't be a surprise, would it?"

"C'mon! Don't fool around. What is it?"

But Chuck refused to say.

"Just follow me."

Jiff looked at Guy and shrugged.

"Might as well humor 'em."

To their surprise, Chuck led them away from the neighborhood and into the woods at the end of Desrosiers Street.

"Out there?" asked Jiff.

Chuck didn't say anything as he proceeded to hop the wooden fence that marked the end of the street. On the other side, he paused to look back the way they'd come.

"What's wrong?" asked Guy.

"Just checkin' to make sure no one sees us," said Chuck. "Don't want anyone followin', especially them girls. Well, Theo would be okay."

Neither Jiff nor Guy said anything. They understood.

Satisfied, Chuck turned and began to follow the trail that led to fern alley and then the stand of distant pine trees marking the foot of Lookout Hill.

"I still don't get it," said Jiff. "What surprise could be in here?"

"Dunno," replied Guy. "I thought I knew every foot of this place."

Soon, they left the bright sunshine of the summer day and stepped into the cool shadows beneath the pines and made their way up hill where the trees gave way to the grassy slope leading to the top. There, the view hadn't changed. Beneath a blue sky dappled with puffs of white clouds, the city of Lowell with its old red brick mills and towering smokestacks spread out across the Merrimack River and the distant neighborhoods of Dracut were just visible in the opposite direction.

"Well?" asked Jiff, growing impatient.

"Hold your horses," said Chuck, moving over to where a flat rock stuck out from the brow of the hill.

Getting on his knees, Chuck pulled at the rock and then flipped it over. Guy and Jiff could only stare.

"What're you doin'?" laughed Jiff. "Lookin' for worms?"

Just then, Chuck pulled out something wrapped in a brown paper bag, now grimed in dirt.

"What's that?" asked Guy, really curious.

In reply, Chuck stripped the bag away from the contents which were revealed to be small box and a glass bottle filled with a greenish liquid.

"A bottle of tonic?" said Jiff. "That's your surprise?"

"You kiddin'?" sneered Chuck. "Haven't you ever seen a wine cooler before?"

"Wine cooler?"

"Sure! It's like regular wine but tastes better 'cause it's got fruit juice mixed in with it. This one's apple flavored."

"Wine?" questioned Guy. The only wine Guy was familiar with was the wine used at church and said so.

"Then you know what I'm talkin' about," said Chuck.

"I do?"

"You must've tasted some of that wine they use?"

Guy was horrified. "Of course not!"

"You must be the only altar boy who hasn't tasted it then."

"No way!"

Chuck just shook his head. "Well, anyway, a wine cooler is the next thing to regular soda pop except it's got a little more kick to it."

Guy said no more, happy to drop the subject. Drink any stronger than coffee was completely absent from his home. His parents never drank any kind of liquor and he was sure Jiff's parents kept only a bottle of wine way up in a kitchen cupboard where no one was able to reach.

"What's in the box?" asked Jiff.

Chuck put down the bottle and fumbled with the box, tearing off its cellophane wrapping. He held it up so the others could see.

"Cherry flavored tiparellos," he exclaimed.

"Cigarettes?" asked Jiff.

"Nah! Cigars. Well, skinny cigars but they have a cherry flavor."

"How'd you know about this stuff?"

"My brother told me about the tiparellos. Let me have a puff of his. And I sneak a swig of the wine coolers my father sometimes leaves unfinished in the 'frig. I asked my brother to get me some of both...don't ask me how he did it! I hid 'em up here so I could surprise you guys. Did I?"

"Yeah," said Jiff. "This is the last thing I'd ever expected to find at the top of Lookout Hill!"

Setting down the cigars, Chuck picked up the bottle and ripped at the paper seal around the cap then popped open the cooler. He took the first sip.

"Ah! Good stuff! And keeping it under that rock kept it cool. Try some." He extended the bottle toward the others.

Jiff and Guy looked uncertainly at each other.

"Go on!"

Warily, Jiff took the bottle and tried a tentative sip.

"Mm," he mumbled, nodding appreciatively.

Chuck smiled and Jiff took another, longer pull.

"It's good," said Jiff, handing the bottle to Guy.

Guy took it and tried a mouthful. It went down easy and didn't taste much different than a soft drink. If there was any alcohol in it, he didn't taste it.

After that, they all sat down in the grass and took turns drinking from the bottle until it was gone.

Next, Chuck picked up the little box and shook out three of the tiparellos. He handed them out to the others and fished out a pack of matches from the bag.

Guy stuck his tiparello into his mouth, getting a feel for the plastic end piece with his lips. Sucking air in through the mouthpiece, he could taste the cherry flavor.

Chuck struck one of the matches and held out the flame to Jiff. Leaning in, Jiff puffed until the tip of his cigar glowed red. A moment later, he was puffing smoke from his mouth.

"Don't breath the smoke into your lungs," cautioned Chuck. "It's not a regular cigarette. You're just supposed to suck it into your mouth and then blow it out."

Next, it was Guy's turn. He had no problem puffing his cigar to life. Now the cherry flavor was stronger and as he blew smoke from his mouth, he thought the whole experience was quite pleasant.

"Ain't this the life?" asked Chuck, as he leaned back and puffed on his own cigar.

"Mm hm," agreed Jiff, doing the same. "Nice."

Guy puffed and watched the smoke he exhaled rise and seem to mingle with the white clouds that skidded across the sky overhead. He did feel somehow content and mellow.

"We should do this more often," suggested Jiff. "It can be our secret."

"And not tell Don and Mike?"

"They're too young," said Chuck with an air of superiority. "Besides, we can't trust 'em not to go blabbin' around about it."

Guy thought about it a moment. "Guess so."

But right there, something in the back of his mind was trying to warn him. Indulging in drink and smoking might have been okay, but what if it was also leading them into betraying their friends?

Something didn't add up, but at the moment, the answer wasn't so obvious.

"I paid my brother for this stuff myself," Chuck was saying. "But if we want more, you guys will have to chip in."

"I don't mind," said Jiff, putting out the rest of his cigar. "What about you, Guy?"

"I don't mind either," said Guy, right away thinking about all of his other expenses. Was it worth sacrificing comic books or books or bike accessories for wine coolers and tiparellos? He didn't think the exchange was a good one but it didn't seem like the right time to contradict the others.

"Okay. When we get some money together, I'll ask my brother to get us some more. We can hide the stuff under this rock and come out here when we want it."

"Sounds good to me," said Jiff.

Guy didn't say anything. Instead, he stood with the others as they made ready to go, and felt like he was going to lose his balance!

"Hey, Guy!" kidded Chuck. "You had too much of that wine cooler?"

So there was enough alcohol content in the drink to effect him, thought Guy.

As the others continued to laugh at Chuck's joke, Guy followed them back down the hill, trying to bring the lightheadedness he felt under control. Luckily, by the time they reached the bottom, the feeling had passed leaving Guy to wonder. The wine cooler had gone to his head, endangering his self control. Was that good? He wasn't sure, but the thought of it left him uneasy...

CHAPTER NINE

In which Guy goes rambling

Nick Tropoli guided the *Attacker*'s shuttle craft to the surface of the big asteroid. He was angry because Buster had placed him in an awkward position. He had left the *Attacker* with an improper pass to do some solo exploring. As the ship's second in command, it was his duty to find Buster, return him to the ship, and throw him in the brig until his case could be reviewed by the commander. It was a duty he hated to do but it had to be done.

What was it about Buster that had always made Nick nervous? Was it his playing fast and loose with the rules? Was it because he never seemed to take his duties seriously? He and Dan had been drawn into trouble more than once because of Buster, once it having cost Nick a year's delay in graduating from the academy. Why did he put up with him? Why did he not just break off the friendship? Even now, this latest stunt was likely to draw Nick onto the bad side of the commander.

The problem with doing the wrong things was that a lot of the time, you never realize that what you're doing is wrong. When you're doing it, it just seems like fun. You don't think ahead to consider any consequences. You never think of putting yourself in the place of a person you might be hurting by your actions.

And Buster never thought of those things. He still acted like a kid and not an adult. An attitude that would only get him into real trouble some day.

Gateway to the Future
Guy DeMonde

"There is nothing wrong with your television set. Do not attempt to adjust the picture. We are controlling transmission. If we wish to make it louder, we will bring up the volume. If we wish to make it softer, we will tune it to a whisper. *We* will control the horizontal. *We* will control the vertical. We can roll the image; make it flutter. We can change the focus to a soft blur or sharpen it to crystal clarity. For the next hour, sit quietly and we will control all that you see and hear. We repeat: there is nothing wrong with your television set. You are about to participate in a great adventure. You are about to experience the awe and mystery which reaches from the inner mind to...the outer limits!"

No matter how many times Guy listened to those words, they never failed to send shivers of anticipation down his spine!

They were the opening words to the *Outer Limits* TV show, the one that he'd missed completely when it was on at night when first broadcast because of his father's homework rule. But now that the series was canceled, it was being rerun on Saturday afternoons and he and Jiff were hooked on its odd combination of gothic science fiction stories.

"I hope it's a good one this week," said Guy.

"Yeah, like the one they had last time about the guy who evolves and grows a sixth finger," recalled Jiff.

"That was a cool episode," agreed Guy. "Or the one about the guy trapped in a spooky house with a monster in the attic!"

"I loved that one!"

The two boys were sitting on the rug in the Jorgenson's TV room only a few feet separating them from the portable television set with its rabbit ear antennae sticking out at odd angles.

Outside, it was a beautiful sunny day, but compared to the *Outer Limits*, it held no immediate attraction for the boys.

"Why don't you boys go out and play," Mrs. Jorgenson was saying from the kitchen. "It's so nice out."

"After the *Outer Limits*, mom," replied Jiff.

It was true that they'd been indoors for most of the afternoon already, having just finished that week's *Fantasmic Features* which ran old monster movies. Scenes from *It, The Terror From Beyond Space* were still fresh in their minds and would provide all the fuel their imaginations needed when they finally ventured back outdoors to reenact them in the yard.

"Where's Chuck been lately?" asked Guy as they waited through a commercial break.

"Think he's gone to his cousin's house in New Jersey for a few days."

"Oh, yeah. Forgot about that."

Guy thought a moment more before continuing, lowering his voice so Mrs. Jorgenson' wouldn't hear.

"Whaddaya think about his brother?" he asked cautiously.

"Chuck's brother? What about him?"

"Well, seems to me his brother isn't like the other big kids around here," said Guy.

"Like how?"

"Well, like how he doesn't hang around with the other big kids."

"So?"

Guy scooched a little closer to Jiff.

"So the other guys don't smoke an' stuff."

"That's what's buggin' ya?"

"Well...seems to me that Chuck's brother isn't...well, good."

"Waddaya mean?"

"You know what I mean."

Jiff shrugged. "I guess I do, but so what? Nothin' wrong with smokin' an drinkin'. Lots of guys do that."

"Your brother doesn't."

"My brother is on the baseball team."

"Yeah, but Chuck's not some guy. He's just a kid, like us. How many kids you know who smoke an' drink?"

Jiff was silent then, thinking.

"Well, what's so bad about smokin' an' drinkin'? Ain't hurt us any has it?"

"Noooo," admitted Guy, hesitantly.

"So what're you fussin' about?"

"Well, if it isn't so bad, how come we need to keep it a secret?"

"Hm. Since you put it that way..."

But time had run out. The program had started and all their attention was immediately drawn to the day's episode of the *Outer Limits*.

After the show was over, Jiff and Guy retreated to the Jorgenson's front porch, imagining they were in a space ship on Mars and while they were out exploring, an unknown creature had slipped through an open hatch. But before they were able to take off again with the creature still on board, Guy's mother was calling him to come home for supper.

"Rats!" he said, getting up from the ship's controls.

"See you later, Guy," said Jiff. "We'll finish later."

"Can't," said Guy. "Have to do my paper route."

"Oh, yeah. I forgot."

"But maybe I can get back in time to play some more before kick the can."

Guy didn't really believe it though. By the time he returned the mood would have left them and Jiff would be in the middle of something else with Mike or Don.

At home, Guy wolfed down his meal and blasted back outdoors again even before his father had time to warm up the ice cream truck for his evening route.

Hopping onto his stingray, Guy took off in the direction of Blazon's Florist to grab his papers. Luckily, it being Saturday, the paper would be the lightest edition of the week so delivery wouldn't be so bad. He could stuff all of his papers in his baskets at once and have no need to make return visits to the corner. Of course, he'd pay for it the next morning when the super fat Sunday papers came out.

Luckily, he managed to avoid both the punk kid he hated and the man eating dog to make it home in good time for kick the can.

He found the others in the Therriens' yard waiting for dusk to fall.

"Made it," he said, throwing himself down on the grassy slope with the others. Nearly everyone else was already there: Jiff, Don, Mike, Polly, Theo, Trece, and Marie.

"Are Toby and Jeannette around tonight?" he asked.

"Nope," replied Don.

"So this is all we've got to play?" For kick the can, the more kids there were, the more fun it was.

"Unless the big kids want to play."

"I doubt it," said Polly. "Butch and Lewis are doing something at school and..."

"...and Percy and Sarah are out on a date!" whispered Theo.

"They are not!" said Don.

"Are too!"

"Are not!"

"Then what do you call it?"

"They're just up at the high school watching the basketball game."

"Together?"

Don shrugged.

"By themselves?"

"I guess so."

"I call that a date," concluded Theo.

The other girls nodded in agreement.

"Looks to me like we won't be havin' them around to play ball or kick the can much longer," said Jiff.

"Whadaya mean?" asked Mike.

"Same thing happened with my big brother and Lewis' brother, Tom. "One day they're foolin' around, tossin' the ball to each other in the street, and the next, it's cars and girls."

"Sad," said Mike.

Just then, the first fireflies started appearing, flitting with their lights going on and off intermittently in the gloom over the field next door. Overhead, the first stars began to twinkle and the lights on the corners of the Therriens' house were on.

"Guess it's dark enough now to get started," said Jiff.

Everyone stood up and gathered in a circle, their fists thrust outward.

"One potato, two potato..." began Jiff, striking fists with his own as he recited the familiar litany.

"Rats!" said Mike.

When Jiff had finished, Mike had ended up being "it."

"Why do I always end up being it first?"

"Not always," observed Marie.

"Almost!"

Resigned, Mike walked over to the inverted Maxwell House coffee can set up in the middle of Don's backyard. Placing his foot on the can, he closed his eyes and began to count.

Instantly, everyone else scattered to their favorite hiding places. Guy and Jiff however, melted into the darkness behind the Cardonas' house and slipped out into Desrosiers Street. Technically, it was against the unspoken rules to leave the area of the Therriens and Cardonas' yards, but the two boys rationalized that their intention was only to circle around and reenter the play area from the other side of the field. Quickly, they ran down the street to the Ohlenbeck's house, directly across from the DeMondes'. There, they sneaked past the picket fence into the back yard then scrambled over a stone wall in the next property where Toby and Jeannette Van der Sands' grandmother lived.

"Is the coast clear?" asked Guy, as they paused on the wall.

Jiff peered past the darkened field to the Therriens' house in the distance. There, Mike could be seen pacing up and down along the back side of the house, staying within the islands of light provided by the outdoor lights, cautiously extending his area of search wider and wider. Already, he'd found Trece and Don who were sitting on the back steps waiting for the round to end.

Cautiously, Guy and Jiff left the wall and rock climbed their way up another atop which was the end of a driveway. Turning around, they sat down, their legs dangling over the side of the wall and leaned into the metal railing that guarded the end of the driveway.

"Wonder how long it'll take for Mike to catch everyone?" asked Guy.

"I think we got a few minutes...oh, look! There goes Theo going for the can!"

It was true. As he watched, Guy saw Theo sneak from around the corner of the house and creep slowly down the slope to the edge of light. Waiting until Mike had gone to the furthest extent of his search pattern, she dashed out of the darkness and kicked the can long before Mike could get there.

"Safe!" she yelled so loud that Guy and Jiff could hear her plainly from where they were.

"Gotta admit," said Jiff. "Theo's a real ball of fire."

"No argument there," agreed Guy, who couldn't help comparing the outgoing Theo to his own sisters. "Think we've made Mike wait long enough?"

"Guess so," said Jiff, slipping from under the railing and falling to his feet below the wall.

Guy did the same and followed Jiff along the chain link fence behind the Beaudoins' house to the corner of the Cardonas' yard, just outside the circle of light surrounding the Therrien's backyard. Though they were not more than thirty feet from the can, they were invisible in the darkness.

Finally, when Mike had once again gone as far as he dared from the can, Jiff ran out and kicked the can so hard that Guy had a hard time finding where it landed in order to kick it himself! As it was, both he and Mike ended up looking desperately for it in the darkness but luckily, Guy found it first and declared himself "safe!"

And so it went for the next couple hours and a dozen rounds. Guy counted himself lucky again for not having to be it more than once. Lucky too in that despite the streetlight in front of the Jorgenson's going on soon after play had begun, he and his sisters weren't expected to rush right back home. It was summer vacation after all and their mother knew exactly where they were.

But all good things must eventually end, and when the mosquitoes became too much to bear, it was mutually agreed to call things off. With a series of "goodbyes," "good nights," and "see ya tomorrows," the gang drifted off in different directions.

But for Guy, the day wasn't yet over. After he and his siblings had taken their baths and made ready for church the next morning, they watched some television before retiring for the evening. As usual, Mr. DeMonde stayed up to watch the late news. Soon enough however, the house had gone dark and quiet for the night.

Guy lay in his darkened room, hands behind his head, waiting for his brothers to fall asleep. It didn't usually take long and it didn't this time. Slowly, he eased himself out of bed and tip toed over to the desk under the window. From there, he could see out over the back yard to the rear of Mike's house and the Jorgenson's field and the brook beyond. It was a clear night with a half moon in the sky.

Guy breathed deep of the fresh night air and listened to the sound of millions of crickets as they filled the night with their chirps. *Time to get to work.* Turning on a lamp to its lowest intensity, he removed a writing pad from the desk and began to reread what he'd written the night before.

After months of thinking about it, he'd finally forced himself to try writing a real story. It'd be filled with adventure and alien planets and romance, just like books by Edgar Rice Burroughs. But unlike those, his novel would be straight out science fiction instead of adventure. Over the previous few months, he'd become used to the unlikely idea that he could be a writer too, just like his favorite authors and came up with some ideas. He wrote an outline of all the chapters and began writing the first only a couple weeks before. Now, reading over what he'd written laboriously in long hand, he was satisfied with his work. He hadn't told anyone what he was doing, not even Jiff. He wanted to convince himself that his desire to write was real, that he intended to pursue it, before he let anyone know. It'd be pretty dumb to tell people that he was a writer only to get tired of it and quit before he could even produce any results.

Placing the pad down on the desk, he picked up a pencil and continued to write...

It was a few days later. Guy and Jiff were crawling in the dark under the Jorgenson's front porch. It was something they used to do all the time when they were kids but hadn't for a long time.

"Let's see if we can still do it," Jiff had said.

"Think we can still fit through the holes?" asked Guy, staring at the small, square opening that gave access beneath the porch. Stooping down, he peered inside and could barely see the light entering from the opposite end where the other opening was.

"Scared?"

"'Course not! I'm just remembering all the spider webs hanging in there..."

"I'll go first," volunteered Jiff.

Getting down on his hands and knees, he squeezed through the hole and disappeared.

"C'mon!" he called, his voice muffled.

Guy stooped and poked his head in the opening. It was dark inside and he needed to wait a few seconds until his eyes adjusted. "Oh, there you are."

Jiff had scooted over some to give Guy room to come through.

Soon, Guy was lying on his belly beside his friend, old wooden boards lay on the dirt floor between them. The smell was musty and Guy was sure the Jorgenson's cat Fluffy had been using the spot to relieve itself.

"Yuch! Spider webs," said Guy, brushing some away from his head.

"C'mon," said Jiff, let's make our way down to the other end."

Together, the boys wormed their way along the length of the long porch, Guy picking up a splinter from one of the old boards along the way. They were all that was left of the frames of the old screens that used to fit around the porch but that Mr. Jorgenson had decided not to bother with. Finally, dusty and filthy from the crawl, they reached the distant hole and Guy wasted no time in squirming his way out, tumbling past the shrub that masked the hole and out onto the fresh, clean grass.

"What're you guys doin'?" said Chuck, hands on hips.

"Huh? Chuck? What are you doin' here?" asked Guy in turn, rubbing dirt from his grimy face.

"Chuck's back?" asked Jiff, still only half way out of the opening. "How was New Jersey?"

"Not bad. More fun in a lot more ways than bein' here."

"Whadaya mean?" asked Guy, defensively. So far as he was concerned, their own neighborhood was plenty fun.

Chuck shrugged and spit. "Well, for one, there're a lot more kids like us there. My cousin even had a gang. Not like UNCLE and THRUSH that we have here, a real gang. One that he had to be initiated to join."

"Ah, you're pullin' our legs," said Jiff dismissively.

"Don't believe me, huh?"

"What was his initiation?" Guy wanted to know.

"He had to steal somethin'."

"Like what?"

"Just anythin'. Just so long as he stole it."

"So he didn't tell you what he stole, huh?" There was still a trace of doubt in Jiff's voice.

"He stole a knife," said Chuck. "All the gang members had knives. Like this one."

Chuck pulled out a folding knife from his pocket, touched a hidden stud, and the blade popped out.

"Wow!" exclaimed Jiff, impressed. "Lemme see it."

"I didn't steal mine," Chuck explained. "On account I wasn't joining the gang. But as long as I was gonna hang around with 'em, I figured I should get one too."

"This is cool," said Jiff, swishing the knife around.

"Careful," cautioned Guy, stepping away to keep out of range.

"Okay, let me have it," said Chuck, extending his hand.

Jiff handed back the knife, not without some reluctance. "Has my slingshot beat all hollow!"

"I think my cousin's gang would've thought your slingshot cool," said Chuck.

"Ya think so?"

"What else was so fun over there?" Guy wanted to know.

"We got to stay up and watch the late show every night. My cousin's father wasn't too strict about that. After he and my father went to bed, me and my cousin stayed up to watch TV as late as we wanted to."

"No kiddin'?"

"And we went to eat a lot of the time at a place called McDonald's."

"Never heard of it."

"It's not like your regular sit down restaurants," said Chuck. "You can get a hamburger, french fries, and a shake for less than a dollar so me and my cousin went there all the time."

"By yourselves?"

"Sure, by ourselves. Wish they had one of those places here."

"What else?"

146

In reply, Chuck glanced up at the window in the back of the Jorgenson's house to make sure no one was there. Then he lowered his voice and whispered "Did some smokin'. Real smokin'."

"Cigarettes?"

"Sure," said Chuck with an air of superiority. "All the gang smoked."

"Huh. Anythin' else?"

"Ramblin'."

"Huh?"

"What?"

"Ramblin'," he repeated.

"What's that supposed to mean?" asked Guy.

Chuck signaled for them to sit down, out of range of the window.

"It's one of the things that the gang liked to do," he whispered. "Most nights, after the late show, me and my cousin would make sure my father and uncle were asleep and we'd sneak out of the house through the bathroom window."

"No kiddin'?" said Jiff, hanging on Chuck's every word.

"No kiddin'" repeated Chuck. "The window wasn't far from the ground so we could just drop down then sneak up the alley. We'd meet the rest of the gang up the street and from there, we'd go ramblin'."

"So what's ramblin'?" persisted Guy.

"Just walkin' around at night, ducking outta sight whenever a cop car came along the street," said Chuck. "Sometimes we'd go to an all night store and buy some near beer..."

"What's that?"

"Tastes like real beer but isn't," explained Chuck. "Then we'd walk around town lookin' for anything that might catch our interest. It was a blast walkin' around in the dark when everybody else is asleep."

"Sounds like fun," said Jiff.

"It was. We'd walk around for a few hours before sneaking back into the house while it was still dark."

"Why don't we try it?" asked Jiff.

"Sneak out in the middle of the night?"

"Sure! I'll bet I could just walk out the cellar door easy," said Jiff. "I could get up in the middle of the night and if anyone sees me goin' downstairs, I could just say I'm goin' to the bathroom."

Guy thought for a moment. "Guess I could climb out my bedroom window onto the shed roof."

"Now you guys are talkin'!"

Despite an uneasy suspicion that once again, he might be doing something not quite on the up and up, Guy rationalized sneaking out of house by reminding himself that he was doing something of the kind already.

He'd discovered early on that going to the Lowell Sun's accounting offices on Saturday morning to pay his paper route bill was a huge bother. By nine o'clock in the morning, the office was jammed with scores of kids all crowding the counters trying to count out their money and settling accounts with the office. It took over an hour for Guy to finish his business there all the while worried about the safety of his bike in the downstairs hallway.

To beat the crowds, he took to going as early in the morning as possible which meant leaving his house before dawn in order to get to the office when it opened at five o'clock. No worries about his bike then nor about crowds. He was the only person at the office and in addition, he'd discovered Dana's Fruitland, a store downtown that sold comic books that he'd drop into on the way home.

But getting out of his house wasn't that easy. His mother was a light sleeper and if the floor squeaked under his feet just a little, she'd wake up and demand to know who was there. Guy had to identify himself and she'd send him back to bed to wait another chance. Funny, though. He'd never considered going out by way of his bedroom window. He always went out by the cellar. Going by the window should take care of his mother finding out what he was doing.

Anyway, seeing that it was still dark out in either case, sneaking out at one or two o'clock wasn't too much different than sneaking out at five was it?

"Let's do it tonight," suggested Jiff, anxious to try the new venture.

"I'm game," said Chuck, who could probably leave his house at any hour he wanted and his father would only ask him what time he'd be back.

"How 'bout you Guy?" asked Jiff.

Guy shrugged. "Sure."

"Okay, then it's settled," said Chuck. "We do it tonight. When do ya wanna do it?"

"One o'clock?" suggested Jiff. "Don't wanna make it too late. I might not be able to stay awake any longer than that."

"Good idea."

"I think everybody oughtta be asleep at my house by then," said Guy.

"Great!" said Chuck. "Where do we meet? I think Jiff's back yard might be best. The streetlights don't reach back there."

Both Jiff and Guy nodded.

"Then we can figure out where we wanna ramble to," concluded Chuck.

"Hey, wait a minute," said Guy. "What about Mike and Don?"

"Do ya wanna bring 'em in on this?"

"Sure, why not?" asked Guy, resentful whenever the others seemed to want to cut their other friends out of their activities.

"Okay, but since it's your idea, you ask 'em," said Jiff.

"I will."

Later that night, Guy lay awake in bed, listening to his brothers' regular breathing, waiting for the glow-in-the-dark arms on his alarm clock to indicate one o'clock. Just then, they showed half past midnight and he was sure the rest of the family was deep in sleep...accept for his mother. But in her case, he was sure that with the bedroom door closed, she wouldn't hear him lift the screen on the window and slip outside.

With nothing to think about but the plan to go rambling, Guy couldn't shake the feeling that once again Chuck was drawing he and Jiff into something shady. Chuck was a good guy and a friend but Guy couldn't help thinking about his unorthodox family, the loose rules of his household, and the influence of his older brother who'd continued to supply them with wine coolers and tiparellos. Certainly, rambling sounded like fun but the fact that in order to do it, he had to do it without his parents' knowledge made him uneasy. He kept telling himself that there was no harm in it. It was just he and his friends enjoying a summer night when all the rest of the world was asleep.

Having eased his conscience, he checked the alarm clock again and this time, it was close enough to one o'clock to get going.

Throwing the covers to the side, he sat up in bed, careful to avoid any squeaking of the mattress. His brothers didn't stir. Slowly, carefully, he began to get dressed and when he was through, tip toed over to the window. There, he lifted the screen and crawled out onto the shed roof. Turning, he lowered the screen, but not all the way in order to keep it from locking in place.

Satisfied, he looked over to Jiff's yard and imagined his friend waiting there in the dark for him. He lowered himself from the shed and hopped the back yard fence into Mike's yard.

"That you, Guy?" someone whispered from the dark.

"Yeah," replied Guy. "Guess you got out okay?"

"I went out by my bedroom window and down off the cellar door roof," said Mike, looking back the way he'd come. "Lumped up my bed to make it look like I'm still there in case my mother comes in to check."

"Good idea," said Guy, thinking that he should have done the same thing.

By now, the excitement of the adventure was taking hold, and he'd forgotten all about his earlier misgivings.

Jiff was waiting for them when they arrived.

"Any trouble getting out?" whispered Guy.

"Nah," said Jiff. "But where's Chuck?"

"Right here," said Chuck, emerging from the darkness. "Everybody here?"

He counted noses. "So Don didn't change his mind?"

"Said it'd be too hard to sneak out," said Guy.

"Okay, then. Let's start ramblin'."

"Where we goin'?" Mike wanted to know.

"Why don't we head down Lakeview?" suggested Chuck, which Guy understood to be the little downtown of Centralville where he delivered his papers. "It's more like the neighborhoods where my cousin's gang would ramble."

"Okay."

Together, they left Jiff's back yard and followed Dean Avenue down to Lakeview. There, the normally busy street was as dead as a cemetery. Nothing stirred. The only sound was the occasional call of a night bird somewhere off in the dark. It was a lonely sound.

"This is weird," said Mike of the quiet, where only occasional streetlights created pools of light that they avoided in order not to be seen if any police car passed. "It feels like we're the last people left alive."

"Yeah, like that movie we saw at the Strand, *The Last Man on Earth*," said Guy.

"You said it," said Jiff, not without a bit of nervousness in his voice.

"You get used to it," assured Chuck, hands jammed in his pockets.

"Got your knife?" asked Jiff.

"Right here," replied Chuck. "Wouldn't go ramblin' without it."

"How far we goin'?" asked Mike.

"Dunno. How far you wanna go, Guy?"

"Let's go to Marie's then cut up Osgood then to Hildreth before coming back around to Pleasant Street," said Guy. Walking up the lonely street was making him nervous. *What if Ma gets up and checks my room?* he wondered. Cutting the ramble off at Marie's Variety store and circling back would ensure that with every step they took, they were actually headed back home.

"Sounds like a plan," said Chuck at Guy's suggestion.

When they reached Marie's, the store was closed. None of them expected it to be otherwise.

"Guess we ain't gonna get any near beer this trip," joked Chuck.

The others laughed as they took the turn onto Osgood. There, the street stretched far ahead into Dracut, both sides of the street lined with cars.

"Watch this," said Chuck, approaching one of the parked cars.

As they walked past, Chuck casually threw his arm over and hooked the radio antennae in his elbow. He kept walking and as he did so, snapped the aerial clean off.

"What'd you just do?" asked Jiff.

"What'd it look like I did?"

"Lemme see that again."

So Chuck did it again a few cars down. "Simple," he said.

"Is that something they did in New Jersey?" asked Mike.

"Yup. Did it all the time. Then we'd read about it in the paper the next day. Everybody was wonderin' who mighta done it. Every car on a street would have their antenna's ripped off. The gang got a kick out of readin' in the paper how the police had no idea who did it. 'Course, they'd cool it for a few days before trying it again somewhere else."

"Jiff!" said Guy. "Did you just…"

"It was easy as pie," said Jiff.

"Lemme try."

As the group walked up the middle of the street, Guy hooked his arm and snapped an antennae right off.

"See how easy it is?" asked Chuck.

Next, it was Mike's turn.

After that, they took turns snapping antennas all the way up the street.

"We better cut it for now," advised Chuck. "Save some for another night!"

"Here come some headlights!"

Quickly, they all dashed onto the sidewalk and crouched behind a parked car.

Slowly, a police car drove past. They watched it until it disappeared around a corner way down the street.

"That was close," said Guy, his heart still pounding.

The rest of the ramble was taken up simply enjoying the silent coolness of the night and by the time they returned to Desrosiers Street, they were ready to turn in.

"We should do this again tomorrow," enthused Mike.

"Tomorrow?" asked Guy.

"Sure," said Chuck.

"Think it's safe to do it every night? I mean, sooner or later our luck's gonna run out and someone's gonna find our beds empty."

"Maybe," said Chuck. "If it happens, it happens. But it might never happen."

Guy had to admit that so far, everything had gone smoothly so he agreed to do it again the next night.

They whispered their farewells and Guy accompanied Mike back to his house before hopping the back yard fence and using a lawn chair to get back up onto the shed. The window screen came up silently enough and when Guy was back inside his room, he found everything as he'd left it. *Whew!*

Getting into his pajamas and resetting the alarm clock, he hoped he'd be able to get up the next morning to serve the early Mass at church. The irony of serving as an altar boy right after committing acts of clear vandalism would occur to him only later. Just then, he was too tired to contemplate such things and fell asleep almost as soon as his head hit the pillow...

CHAPTER TEN

*In which Guy takes a stand
and cherishes a secret*

As executive officer aboard the *Attacker,* Nick had had to do a number of things he did not like including disciplining crew members who violated ship's protocol or the commander's orders.

For the most part, he was able to do it without becoming emotionally involved as they say. But more often than most, he found himself having to deal with Buster. He considered him his friend and for a long time he brushed off his antics as just innocent hijinks. But lately, Buster's offenses had become more serious and Nick was forced to decide between friendship or the good of the Space Force.

He chose the Space Force.

Gateway to the Future
Guy DeMonde

Soon after Guy had returned from his regular summer vacation in Salem and Jiff had come back from his trip to Alabama (with more stories about he and Alice that somehow made Guy feel jealous), UNCLE had another run-in with THRUSH.

Guy didn't remember what started it this time because all he could think about was that Rocky was back with THRUSH.

"You sure that kid's a friend of yours?" asked Chuck as each gang faced off on opposite sides of the Beaudoins' fence.

"Everywhere but here, I guess," replied Guy, recalling how he and Ricky had just been over to Rocky's the other day to help clean out his shed. It was funny how they could be friends at school but here, be adversaries.

Just now, both sides confronted each other, waiting for someone to make the next move.

As usual, Lester was ready with stuff to throw. This time, it was rotten tomatoes from the Toussain's garden.

"Well, what's it gonna be?" demanded Bobby.

"Yeah, we can't stand around here all day," said Deni.

Lester threw one of his tomatoes at Don but Don dodged it easily.

"Anything you want," called Jiff. "Name it!"

Unfortunately, Jiff's challenge was just the opening the others were waiting for.

"Okay, Rocky versus Guy," said Bobby, smirking.

"Whadaya mean by that?" asked Jiff.

But Guy already knew and wondered whose idea it had been to match him up with Rocky. Was it a loyalty test to join THRUSH? Suddenly, he knew why THRUSH had initiated the confrontation in the first place.

"We wanna find out if Rocky can stand up to one of you guys," said Bobby. "We asked 'em who he wanted to fight and he picked Guy."

Jiff looked at Guy. "You know anything about this, Guy?"

Guy shook his head, as confused as Jiff was. "No!"

"You wanna go through with it?"

How could Guy turn down the challenge without besmirching the honor of UNCLE, let alone himself? He had to accept the challenge.

"I'll do it."

"You heard 'em," Jiff told Bobby. "We'll meet ya at my house in five minutes."

"Okay. C'mon, fellas." Slowly, the others turned away with Lester backing up, tomatoes ready in his hands to cover their retreat if necessary.

A few minutes later, Guy, Jiff, Chuck, Mike, and Don were gathered in Jiff's front yard, waiting for THRUSH.

"Can you handle 'em, Guy?" Chuck was asking.

"Sure I can," replied Guy although he wasn't as confident as he sounded. He knew Rocky was a faster runner in the games of relievio they played in the school yard and that he was slightly taller. Could he take him?

"Remember, don't use your fists," advised Jiff. "That'll just give Rocky an excuse to do the same."

"Yeah, much better just to keep to wrestling," agreed Don. "Then just pin his shoulders back."

Fists? Guy hadn't even considered that! In contests with THRUSH, their fights never involved fists, only wrestling. Would Rocky try to punch him? He found that hard to believe.

Just then, Bobby, Deni, Lester, Normy, and Rocky stepped out of the woods at the end of the street and advanced past Guy's house to the Jorgenson's yard. In another few minutes, the two sides faced each other over Jiff's front lawn.

"No fists," said Jiff impulsively.

Bobby shrugged. "Fine by me. Rocky?"

"No problem. I'll beat 'em easy no matter what."

Guy said nothing.

Just then, Rocky lunged forward and next thing Guy knew, he found himself back peddling across the yard. Before he could gather his wits, he fell backward with Rocky on top of him. Something had been jarred loose in his mouth and he called out "Wait! Wait a minute!"

"What's wrong, Guy? Already calling uncle?"

The others laughed at the unintended pun.

"No! I think I just lost a tooth."

Guy put a finger in his mouth and sure enough, found a tooth that had been knocked out when he fell backward.

"So you gonna use that as a cheap excuse to stop the fight?" asked Rocky from where he straddled Guy's stomach.

In response, Guy surged up and threw Rocky off and together, they began to roll around on the lawn, each trying to pin the other down and declare victory.

Meanwhile, everyone else stood back and watched; but except for Lester urging Rocky to greater effort, no one really did any cheering.

In their struggle, Guy and Rocky neared the hedges that grew atop the low wall that bordered the front yard.

"Hey, watch out for the hedges!" warned Jiff. "If you wreck 'em, my mother's gonna kill me!"

He would have interfered with the fight but his arms were pinned by Bobby from behind.

"Let 'em go," said Bobby. "We don't need any excuses to stop 'em."

"It's not an excuse," insisted Jiff, struggling to free himself. "Guy's doin' all right."

Just then, Guy and Rocky did what Jiff had feared: rolling over, they crashed through the hedges, bending and mangling a good three feet of them, before tumbling over the wall. Then, as if by mutual consent, they stopped fighting and stood up.

"Had enough?" asked Guy, spitting some blood caused by his missing tooth.

"Have you?" returned Rocky, who was scruffed up with some scratches on his face from rolling over the hedges.

"Okay, let's get outta here," said Bobby, releasing Jiff. "Rocky's proved himself."

As the THRUSH agents left the yard and made their way back to the end of the street, his friends gathered around Guy.

"That was a good fight, Guy," congratulated Don.

"Yeah! Good job! You showed them," agreed Mike.

"You've got more moxie than I thought," said Chuck, clapping Guy on the shoulder.

"What about that tooth?" asked Jiff from where he was trying to straighten out the mangled hedges. "Does it hurt?"

Guy shook his head. "Nah. It was loose anyway."

Despite the general consensus that UNCLE had won, there was something about this latest encounter that left a bad taste in their mouths. Unlike past battles, there hadn't been any fun in it. This time, it'd been deadly serious. As a result, though they didn't realize it at the time, it would mark the end of the war between the two sides.

Meanwhile, during the week that he'd been gone to Salem, Guy's sisters had taken over his paper route and seemed to have had no problems with it, not even from the punk kid. Guy figured that even the punk balked at trying to give girls any trouble.

Punk kids were becoming an increasing problem for Guy. Besides the one on his paper route, there were whole neighborhoods of them deeper in Lowell on the far side of Centralville where he'd discovered Leo's Self Serve, another variety store that had a spinner rack jammed with comics. Although he still gave his primary loyalty to Hovey's, he had to admit that Hovey's had only a limited assortment of comics compared to Leo's and sometimes it didn't get all the comics that Guy was expecting. To find the missing titles, he had begun to look for other stores that sold comics and found Leo's on his way to the *Lowell Sun* when he went to pay his paper route bill. The only problem was that it was smack dab in the center of the roughest neighborhood in Centralville. Luckily however, Guy had noticed that the area was dead early in the morning (punk kids were notoriously late sleepers) so he could continue passing through on the way downtown.

Even luckier was the day he'd discovered Dana's Fruitland! He'd ignored the store at the beginning whenever he passed it on the way to the *Sun*. It came after he'd passed Leo's and appeared from the outside to be an unlikely place to sell comics. But one day, lured into the store by the sight of a big grape juice bubbler on the counter, he found out that there was lots more to it than all the bins of fresh groceries, fruit, and vegetables that was all that could be seen from the display windows outside or of the vast variety of cigarettes and cigars arrayed behind the cash counter. Way in the back was a magazine rack at the very bottom of which was a row of comic books.

Now Guy had not one, but three places to check in making sure he could get all of the titles he was expecting each week. More and more, he took to waiting till he could buy his comics at Dana's right after leaving the Sun rather than taking his chances at Hovey's. Furthermore, Dana's also had a spinner rack of paperback books and it was there Guy discovered a series of books by Edmond Hamilton featuring his space faring hero, Captain Future! Guy was hesitant at first to pay full cover price for a new book instead of Harvey's marked down prices for used books, but as soon as he'd read the first chapter of *Calling Captain Future,* he never looked back. He was hooked and had to get all of the volumes in the series.

With the discovery of Dana's, now he could skip the rough neighborhood and its population of punk kids altogether. But in considering the phenomenon of punk kids, Guy was forced to reassess his own friend Chuck. In many ways, he shared characteristics in common with the punk kids that Guy hated including their trademark use of foul language. It had been a wonder that neither he nor Jiff had picked up that particular habit.

Guy had already trained himself out of the spitting habit that he'd picked up from Chuck and wondered if, under different circumstances, would he consider Chuck one of the good kids or a punk? Reluctantly, he was slowly coming to the latter conclusion, what with their continued use of wine coolers and smoking up on Lookout Hill and now their night time ramblings. There was no doubt in his mind that he hated punk kids and wanted nothing to do with them or their nasty doings and yet, when it came to Chuck, he balked.

Those thoughts were still on his mind as he and the others continued to ramble. Sneaking out of the house late at night had become routine with Guy no longer so worried that his absence would be discovered by his parents. Gradually however, the empty streets and dodging police patrols had lost their glamor (as did snapping car antennas) with the boys finding the comfort of their warm beds and a good night's sleep more attractive.

"I'm glad we stopped rambling," said Guy one day. "I was getting tired of being sleepy all day."

"Yeah," agreed Jiff. "My mother was beginning to wonder why I was taking naps every day after lunch."

"You should've did what I did," said Mike, who'd given up on the rambles before the others. "And stopped earlier."

"Maybe we should've," said Guy, sounding out Jiff's feelings on the matter. "I wasn't crazy about snapping those antennas anyway."

"It was fun seeing it in the newspaper though," said Jiff. "The mysterious antenna snappers that the police could never find!"

"You proud of that?" asked Guy without thinking.

Jiff shrugged. "Not proud sorta. Oh, I dunno. I can't explain it."

Guy didn't say anything but he'd already brought it up a couple weeks before when his father took he and his sisters to church for Confession. It was with a real sense of relief that he'd told the priest what he'd done and to be forgiven for it. It was that sense of relief that told him he'd been right to suspect what they were doing was not good. The remaining question was: was drinking wine coolers and smoking tiparellos sinful? The jury was still out with that one.

"Well, I'm glad we stopped goin' out at night," said Guy. "We were pushin' our luck for sure."

"Guess you're right," said Jiff.

They were hanging around in the apple tree in the Jorgenson's back yard. Jiff and Guy sat side by side about half way up the tree while Don hung up side down on a lower branch. Mike was trying to see how far out he could inch along one of the branches before it threatened to snap under his weight. All around them, the apples were slowly changing color from green to red and from all appearances, would make for a bumper crop come September.

"Uh oh," said Guy.

"What?" asked Jiff.

"Here comes Chuck."

Chuck had crossed the street and entered the Jorgenson's field heading straight for the apple tree.

"Why 'uh oh?'" asked Jiff.

"I dunno. Lately I'm startin' not to like Chuck...or his big brother."

"How come?"

"I dunno," said Guy again, not ready to express his real feelings just then. He wasn't even sure about them anyway.

"Hey, fellas!" hailed Chuck. He stopped beneath the tree and stood looking up at the others.

"Hey, Chuck," returned Jiff. "C'mon up!"

Chuck accepted the invitation and began shinnying up the main trunk of the tree and soon was resting on the same branch as Jiff and Guy.

"Move over a little," he said.

"We were just talkin' about rambling," said Jiff.

"What about it?"

"We're tired of it," piped up Mike. "Would rather sleep."

"Softies," said Chuck, trying a bite at one of the apples.

"Sounds like I didn't miss anything," said Don. "I was better off in bed."

"I wouldn't go that far," said Mike as the branch he was walking on suddenly sagged almost to the ground.

"So what're you gonna do Chuck?" asked Jiff. "Still gonna go out even by yourself?"

Chuck spit out the apple mulch he was chewing and threw the remainder of the apple away.

"Still sour," he said. "Nah. No fun ramblin' by myself."

"What're we gonna do now then?" asked Jiff.

"Spy on THRUSH?" asked Mike, stepping off the branch and watching as it snapped back up.

"Nah. I'm done with that stuff," said Chuck. "But it doesn't mean we have to stop."

"Huh? Wadaya mean by that?" asked Guy.

"Was thinkin' a maybe goin down to the park and see what's goin' on down there."

"Which park?" asked Jiff.

"What other park is there around here? St. Louis Park."

"Whaddaya got in mind?" asked Guy.

Chuck shrugged. "My brother says it's a real hoppin' place at night. I thought we might ramble on down there and see if he's right."

"I'm for it," said Jiff eagerly.

"I'll go," said Guy who thought the venture sounded pretty harmless compared to late night rambling.

"What about kick the can?" asked Mike.

"What about it?" asked Chuck.

"When are we gonna play if we're down at the park?"

Chuck laughed. "We don't play, dummy. Who wants to play kick the can when we can go ramblin' down to the park where all the big guys go?"

Mike didn't answer.

"How 'bout you Don? You gonna come?"

Don swung around the branch he'd been hanging from, landing on his feet.

"I'll go," he said. "At least once. But if all we end up doin' is hangin' around, then forget it. I'd rather play kick the can."

Later, after the sun had set leaving a pink smear on the clouds that hung near the western horizon, the gang assembled in front of Jiff's house and walked down Dean Avenue to Lakeview. They followed the same course toward Centralville's business district that they used when they went on their late night rambles.

"Let's stop in to Marie's first," suggested Chuck. "I wanna get a drink."

By the time they reached the little variety store across the street from the park, night had fully fallen. Inside, business was brisk as teenagers and other kids went back and forth from the park to buy bottles of soda, snacks, and candy.

"What're you lookin' for?" asked Guy.

"Near beer," replied Chuck, sticking his head in the store's big refrigerator.

Not interested, Guy instead, scanned the counter where boxes of trading cards were displayed. He had some change in his pocket, enough to buy a few packs of the new Marvel Comics trading cards but decided right then wasn't the time to buy some. They'd have to wait.

There was a commotion behind him and when Guy turned, he saw Chuck holding up a bottle in triumph.

"Found some!" he declared.

"Will they let you buy it?" asked Jiff.

"They're too busy to notice," said Chuck confidently.

He was right. The girl behind the register took his money without a glance at what he was buying.

Outside, Chuck twisted off the cap and took a gulp of the near beer.

"Ah! Not bad!"

"Lemme try," demanded Jiff.

Chuck handed him the bottle and as Jiff gulped said "Hey, take it easy! Here, Guy."

Guy took a gulp but found the taste unpleasant. "Yuch. I'll stick to wine coolers!"

"Wimp!" Chuck laughed.

"Hey, what about us?" asked Don.

"Too young! This stuff'll put hair on your chest!"

"Forget it, Don," soothed Guy. "You're not missin' anything."

"C'mon. Let's go over to the park," said Chuck, leading the way across Lakeview and joining the stream of kids heading in the same direction.

Ahead, brilliant lights mounted on tall poles not only lit the softball field like it was day time, but most of the rest of the park as well. As the gang entered, teenaged boys were sitting along a wooden railing trying to make time with girls while behind them, younger kids amused themselves loudly on ranks of swings and monkey bars.

Everywhere, crowds of people, mostly youngsters, milled about talking, laughing, and shouting.

Further on, members of the local softball league were playing a deadly serious game on the field with the stands crammed with family and friends applauding and cheering them on. Just then, there was a hit and everyone stopped what they were doing to see if the ball would make it over the outfield fence. It didn't, and was caught easily by a player before being thrown back to second to hold the runner at first base.

After watching the play, the boys continued on.

"There's your father, Guy," said Mike, pointing to the Mister Softee truck parked behind home plate. Brightly lit in a bank of fluorescent lights, there was a long line of customers waiting to be served. Frappes and banana boats seemed to be the popular choices for the evening.

"Looks like he's makin' a killin' tonight," said Don.

"He told me this park was a gold mine," said Guy of the carnival atmosphere. "He comes here three or four times a night."

"Looks like he's too busy to ask him for anything," said Jiff.

"Yeah, better not bother him," said Guy.

"Let's go down to the basketball courts," suggested Chuck, swigging from his bottle of near beer and trying hard to look like he was one of the big kids.

There, a number of scratch games were in progress over all of the four courts. All played by bigger guys and some adults.

"Not likely they'd invite us to play," said Don.

"I'm not interested anyway," said Guy. His sportsmanship was embarrassing enough when played among the neighborhood kids. The last thing he wanted was to foul up among a bunch of strangers.

Just then, Guy froze.

Not far away, he saw someone he recognized. It was the punk kid that always bothered him on his paper route! It was then he remembered that the kid's house was adjacent to the park. Of course there'd always been a good chance that he could be here. Why hadn't he thought of that before? He remained frozen, his hands in his pockets, head facing the activity on the basketball court while out of the corner of his eyes, he watched the kid move off in a different direction. *Whew! That was close!*

"What's the matter, Guy?" asked Don. "You look like you saw a ghost."

"Huh? Oh, nothin'. Just thought I saw someone I recognized."

"There's someone you oughtta recognize," said Chuck, gulping some near beer.

"Who?" Sweat suddenly began to roll down his sides as he worried it might be the punk kid.

"Over there. Isn't that Rocky?"

Guy looked and in a moment had picked out Rocky from the crowd.

"Hey! Rocky!" shouted Chuck. "C'mon over here!"

It took a moment for Rocky to figure out who was calling him and when he did, left some other kids and came over.

"What're you guys doin' here?" he said good naturedly. "Spying out the place for UNCLE?"

"Quit with the kid stuff," said Chuck.

"How's your tooth, Guy?" asked Rocky. "Hope you're okay."

"No problem. The new one's already startin' to grow out."

"That was a pretty good fight though, wasn't it?" asked Rocky. "Didn't think you'd be that tough to handle."

Guy shrugged. "Same here. But what I want to know is why'd you switch sides?"

It was Rocky's turn to shrug. "Bobby had a neat clubhouse that's all."

Nothing more needed to be said and they parted amicably.

"See ya in school," said Rocky in parting.

Guy waved him off. "Fifth grade this year if we don't stay back again!"

Rocky laughed and waved back.

"Well, that was disappointing," said Chuck.

"What?"

"Thought we might get a rematch!"

Everybody laughed at that.

For the next hour or so, they continued to wander around the park. Finally, Chuck had finished his drink and was tossing it into an overflowing trash barrel when the roar of the crowd on the viewing stand caught his attention.

Someone had just hit another long one and everyone had stood up, gasping and cheering. As things calmed down again and people resumed their seats, Chuck inclined his chin in their direction.

"Hey, there's some cute girls over there," he said.

"Where?" asked Jiff.

"Sitting on those benches. The second row from the bottom."

Jiff stood on tip toe, craning his neck in the direction Chuck indicated. "Ohhhhh yeaaaah."

Guy looked too and saw a group of three girls sitting together and had to admit they did look attractive.

"Too old," he said. "Must be eighth graders at least."

"So what?" said Chuck, still admiring them. "So long as they're good lookin'. That's what my brother always says."

"Who cares about them?" Mike wanted to know. "We got our own girls back home."

Chuck made a face. "I'm talkin' real girls. Not girls we know. Well, except for Theo."

"What's the difference?" Don wanted to know. He was far more interested in watching the softball game than girl watching.

"If ya don't know, I can't explain it to ya," said Chuck.

When they grew tired of looking at the girls in the stands, they moved on. There was still a long line at the Mister Softee truck so bothering Mr. DeMonde was out of the question. As they passed the truck, Guy was certain that many of those in line were already going for seconds.

"Hold it!" said Chuck suddenly, his arms out to keep the others back. "I think I'm in love!"

The others couldn't help laughing. "What now?"

"You mean who now? Looky over there!"

They looked and Guy's heart leaped.

It was Michelle LaRochelle, a girl in his class. But not just any girl. The one he'd had a secret crush on since staying back and joining her class. She seemed to be walking along toward the softball field with friends but Guy never did remember who the others were. The only one he saw was Michelle, which was the only one Chuck saw too.

"Now there's a cute girl," Chuck was saying.

Instantly, Guy felt the back of his neck grow hot, resenting Chuck's open admiration for Michelle. Why he should feel that way, was puzzling. Guy had no claim on Michelle. In fact, he suspected she didn't even know he existed. But that didn't make any difference. He still felt a proprietary interest in her and resented anyone else, especially Chuck, showing interest.

"Those curls, that smile, those shorts!" said Chuck, as the others laughed.

But inwardly, Guy was steaming. He wanted to tell Chuck off. That Michelle was his by virtue of knowing her first. But he couldn't do it. He was afraid the others would only laugh at him. And so, he just kept quiet, rationalizing that there was no way Chuck could ever progress beyond admiring Michelle from afar. And that as soon as they left the park, she'd be out of his mind.

But seeing Michelle away from school like that, when she wasn't wearing her uniform but instead, in a blouse and shorts and walking along sipping a Coke, made her seem like a completely different person than the one he knew. A more exotic, more exciting person. Unbidden, the memory of that summer in Salem the year before when those girls had kissed him on their front steps and he'd shot up and flew to the sidewalk sprung to mind. He could admit it now. They'd scared him to death! But now, seeing Michelle, and feeling the feelings he was suddenly feeling now, he wondered...would he jump again if *she* ever kissed him?

Such a thought was so thrilling...and frightening in a way, that he quickly dismissed it from his mind. Looking around, he'd hoped none of his friends had read his thoughts. Luckily, they're own thoughts had moved on to something else.

"There's lots of girls down here," Jiff was saying, looking around at the busy park.

"This'll be the place to find 'em when we're ready to look some up," said Chuck.

"I'll make a note of that," said Jiff as they moved along.

"Watch it, Jiff," said Chuck. "You don't want Alice gettin' wind o' that!"

"Alice is way off in Alabama," said Jiff. "Seein' her once a year don't cut it."

Both boys laughed at Jiff's flippancy, but Guy was surprised at his best friend's casual dismissal of a girl he could hardly stop talking about when he arrived home earlier in the summer.

"Guy's been pretty quiet since we saw that pretty one with the shorts," said Chuck, winking. "You like 'er too, Guy?"

Guy shrugged, struggling not to show his interest. "I'll admit, she *was* cute. But there're a lot more fish in the sea!"

"You can say that again," agreed Chuck. "Here comes some more now."

It was with relief that Guy realized that Chuck's interest in Michelle was only a random, fleeting one and not serious. Surreptitiously, when he thought the others weren't paying attention, he looked back to catch a last glimpse of her as she disappeared into the crowd. She might never know of his own admiration for her but that was all right too. It would remain his own cherished secret.

CHAPTER ELEVEN

In which Guy makes a key realization

Things came to a head when Buster was caught pilfering from ship's stores.

Ship's supplies were carefully calculated to last the length of a mission and no longer. Rarely was there room for error in a ship with limited space for storage. And so, anyone taking more than his fair share from such supplies as food and water, would face serious consequences if caught.

Buster, as a second lieutenant, knew that as well as anyone. Nevertheless, as he told Nick, he'd been helping himself to extra rations for months and brushing it off as not important.

"What do a few insta-meals matter?" he asked when Nick had dragged him on the carpet. "We're approaching Earth now and there's going to be plenty of extra."

"You know as well as I do, that doesn't matter," replied Nick, repressing his anger and frustration. "It's the principle of the thing."

"Rules were meant to be broken," said Buster nonchalantly.

It was plain to Nick that Buster was relying on their friendship to skate past any responsibility for his actions.

"Without any remorse, you leave me with no alternative but to cite you for insubordination," said Nick. "On my recommendation, Staff will strip you of your rank and drum you out of the Force."

With that, and an unbelieving look on Buster's face, his former friend was gone and out of his life. It was back to just he and Dan again.

Gateway to the Future
Guy DeMonde

With the end of summer, it was back to school for Guy and his friends. As usual, it took a few days to get used to the old routine at St. Louis Elementary School among which was Guy's continued service as an altar boy. The difference now being that he was a veteran with almost a year's worth of experience.

Halloween and then Christmas seemed to arrive quickly but then everything slowed down through the winter until it seemed as if spring would never come. But finally, it did, as it always had.

"Hard to believe we were like that once," said Ricky, looking on as Pere Andre put the new recruits through their paces. He and Guy were in the sacristy, peeking through the door into the nave, watching as the new kids were shown the proper way to ring the bells during the Offertory.

"Yeah, it seems so long ago now," agreed Guy.

Guy didn't say so, but despite being at it for almost year, he still felt a sense of pride when serving Mass knowing that his classmates were in the congregation at the eight o'clock Mass on Sunday morning. Designated as the "children's Mass," it was when all the grades at school attended and sat not with their families, but grouped with their respective classes.

But for Guy, the only one he cared to be noticed by was Michelle LaRochelle and those times he held the spatula beneath her chin as she knelt to receive communion, he struggled not to show emotion, but to retain the proper air of solemnity. What he really felt though, was a sense of importance that he hoped wouldn't be lost on her. The problem though was that she also seemed to be good at controlling her own emotions so that, back in class, she continued to act as if he was invisible.

"Uh, oh," said Ricky. "I feel sorry for that kid."

One of the recruits had stumbled in his recitation of the Latin prayers indicating he hadn't practiced reading them over the night before.

Guy was currently assigned to serving the early morning Mass on weekdays, just before school started. The good part about it was that he was allowed to enter the first class of the day late with no questions asked. It also contributed to that same sense of importance when he walked into class and found his seat while the other students were already at work.

"I wonder if any of those kids think they're gonna get to serve at funerals right off the bat?" asked Ricky.

"They're gonna be disappointed," said Guy, who'd felt the disappointment himself. He'd never been asked to serve at a funeral in the whole year since becoming an altar boy and so never enjoyed the satisfaction of getting any of the tips they'd heard about when he first joined. Instead, Deni Cardolet seemed to get picked to do all the funerals.

"I've done a few funerals," Ricky was saying, unconsciously challenging Guy's belief. "But so far, I've never gotten any tips."

"Really? I'd thought that Deni would be rich by now with all the funerals he does," said Guy.

"If he's gettin' any tips, I don't know how he does it."

"This is gettin' boring," concluded Guy at length. "Let's go over to your house and do somethin'."

"Okay."

On the way out, they passed through the locker room where Guy made sure his newly dry cleaned cassock and surplice were properly stored. After that, the two boys left the church and walked across the street to Ricky's house, a triple decker that faced the big brick edifice that was St. Louis Elementary School. Ricky's family owned the building and lived on the first floor. Supposedly, Ricky had two older brothers, but Guy had never seen them. They were much older even than the big kids back on Desrosiers Street and might even have been married.

"Wanna play some catch?" asked Ricky.

"Sure."

Despite the still cold temperatures and scatterings of old snow on the ground, Guy had brought the new first baseman's mitt he'd received for Christmas. Digging it out of the basket on his bike, he rammed his fist into the pocket to loosen it up. Ricky returned from the house with an outfielder's mitt and a baseball. They could've played in the street, it was quiet enough, but they preferred the school yard across the street that had plenty more room.

As they began to throw, Guy warmed up enough to discard his coat. Gradually, as their arms limbered up, the two boys increased the distance between them, catching throws that resembled pop flies. Sooner than Guy liked however, Ricky's mother called them to say it was 4 o'clock.

"Rats!" blurted Guy.

"What's the matter?" asked Ricky, joining him as they walked back.

"That paper route is gettin' to be a pain," said Guy.

"Thought you liked it?"

"I like the money."

"Oh. Thinkin' of gettin' rid of it?"

"You interested?"

"Might be."

"I'll stick it out a while longer," said Guy, hopping on his bike. "But I'll let you know if I ever decide to quit."

Which wasn't too likely as he needed the extra money the route gave him to finance his comic book, trading card, and book buying habits. Not to mention trips to the Strand to watch movies and keeping he and Jiff and Chuck in wine coolers.

But now there was another reason to get aggravated: A new soap opera had just debuted on television every day at 4 o'clock, the exact time he had to leave to do his papers. It was called *Dark Shadows* and was broadcast every weekday. Now, Guy wasn't a soap opera fan with those shows' constant romantic complications, but he was interested in anything to do with vampires, and werewolves which was *Dark Shadows'* stock in trade. Most days, he'd manage to stick around home to watch the first half of the show with his sisters and it was all he could do to tear himself away to go to work.

Yeah, this paper route business is for the birds, thought Guy, while also reminding himself of that stupid dog and the punk kid who still annoyed him now and then.

But if Guy was bothered by the demands of his paper route when good weather allowed rapid delivery on his bike, it became much worse when the bad weather set in. Winter came early that year with the first light snowfall taking place before Thanksgiving. But even with only a dusting, the roads and sidewalks were far too slippery and dangerous for a bicycle. And when it rained, plunging temperatures would coat the wet sidewalks in a sheen of ice. Soon enough, he was forced to abandon his bike for the season and deliver his papers on foot. And when that meant going back and forth to the corner to get new armfuls, the time wasted was colossal. Then winter set in making things even worse if that was possible. By then, Guy was thinking seriously of abandoning the route and giving it to Ricky.

But he stuck it out; especially when Saturday mornings arrived and he stopped into Dana's Fruitland and bought the week's new comics and found a new Captain Future book. Then, all of his doubts disappeared and he knew it was worth it...until the next day when he had to deliver the super-fat Sunday editions!

One good thing about the winter though. It meant no more wine coolers and cigars on Lookout Hill. The snow was too deep and hard packed to make it all the way up there. And even if they did, the rock they hid the stuff under was frozen to the ground. The practice of drinking and smoking had long since paled for Guy and he would've dropped the whole thing if it wasn't for Jiff. They were still friends and Guy hated the idea that they could drift apart if he didn't continue to participate. Strangely, he didn't feel the same way at all about Chuck and often wondered why that was. Was Chuck a real friend like Jiff, Mike, and Don were? Or was he simply an acquaintance. Someone from outside who simply drifted into their circle for a while?

Winter's cold also put a stop to rambling, something else Guy was thankful for. He'd long since admitted to himself that snapping those car antennas was a bad thing to do but he was also uncomfortable with their night time walks down to the park. He didn't care for it when Chuck would openly admire the girls and say so right out loud. Guy admitted to himself that he was more on the bashful side when it came to girls, and didn't like it when he had to act differently to keep the others from noticing. Luckily, though, they never again spotted Michelle at the park so he was spared Chuck's disrespectful comments and the fear that he might actually attempt to act on his attraction to her.

And so, the winter drifted on, past Christmas and New Year's into the spring again when Guy finally was able to break out both his sneakers and his bike. With his freedom of movement restored, his complaints about the paper route receded somewhat and things started to get back to normal in the neighborhood.

And one of those signs of normalcy was the family's observance of meatless Fridays. Now sometimes, Guy's father would surprise everyone by getting pizza for supper, but more often his mother would send Guy to the store to get fish. That meant a trip down to the end of Dean Avenue to Bouchard's. Once, before the discovery of Hovey Square Variety, Bouchards had been the focus for every kid in the neighborhood due to its wide selection of penny candy. These days however, Guy only visited there when his mother gave him money to buy fish on Fridays.

Usually, getting the fish was a solitary activity for Guy, but this time, Jiff and Chuck decided to go down with him.

"Nothin' else to do," explained Chuck.

"We haven't been down there in a long time," said Jiff. "I'm curious to find out if anything's changed."

"They're puttin' in a new soda fountain," said Guy.

"No kiddin'? For ice cream and everything?"

"Yeah."

"It might mean competition for your father," said Jiff.

"I never thought of that," admitted Guy.

By that time, they'd reached the end of the street and crossed Sladen Street to the front of the store which sat at the fork of Sladen and Lakeview Avenue.

"Still looks the same from out here," said Jiff, as they mounted the wooden steps to a porch area that fronted the building. The store itself occupied the ground floor of a two story structure whose wooden slats, badly in need of a new coat of paint, made the building look more run down than it was.

Guy pushed in the heavy door and stepped inside where numerous rows of shelving were arranged supermarket fashion. On the right, in front of the display window, sat Miss Bouchard behind the cash register, still overseeing the penny candy counter that was divided into dozens of separate squares each holding different kinds of candy, everything from bazooka bubble gum to wax lips.

"*Bonjour, Madmoiselle Bouchard,*" said Jiff, with a little wave.

"*Bonjour, Guy,*" she replied, pronouncing his name in French.

"Is Mr. Bouchard in back? My mother sent me to get some fish."

"He's there."

"Hey, look at this," said Jiff from the opposite side of the store.

Guy walked over and saw how that side of the store had been cleared away. The frame of a new wooden counter was under construction.

"Is this where the soda fountain is gonna go?"

"Must be," said Guy. "I'm goin' out back."

Guy left the others and made his way down the gloomy center aisle to the deli counter at the rear of the store.

"*Bonjour, mon tit Guy!*" came the hearty greeting from the heavy set man behind the counter whose hams, sausages, and cheeses could barely be seen behind the condensation that smeared the glass display case. "It's Friday so you must be here for some fish."

"Yup. Do you know how much my mother wants too?"

"It's been increasing over the last couple of years so the family must be getting bigger," said Mr. Bouchard, who wore a grease stained apron and white paper hat on his head. "Want to come around and watch me fry it up?"

"Sure!"

Guy rounded the display case and followed Mr. Bouchard into the back room. There, a heavy stove sat with vats of boiling grease on the range. The vats were already filled with pieces of haddock. This was Bouchard's busy day with many families in the neighborhood ordering fish for supper.

"You can help me wrap this stuff up," said Mr. Bouchard, pointing at a big roll of brown wax paper.

Guy knew what he wanted, having done it many times before. He pulled out a good sized sheet of the paper, tore it free and laid it down on a cutting table. Mr. Bouchard then lifted a metal basket from one of the vats and dumped its contents into a big bowl of bread crumbs. After rolling the pieces of fish in the crumbs and making sure they'd been covered all around, he took them out and laid them on the prepared paper. Guy then wrapped the fish in the paper and slipped it into a clean paper bag. Finally, after a few minutes, it was the turn of his mother's own order and when he finished packing up the fish, bid farewell to Mr. Bouchard and headed for the cash register.

Miss Bouchard had just finished ringing up the order when Guy was joined by Jiff and Chuck.

"You guys ready to go?"

"Been ready for the last half hour," said Chuck.

"Get away! It hasn't been that long," chided Guy, heading for the door.

Outside, they crossed Sladen Street and entered Dean Avenue, the freshly fried fish, hot in the crook of Guy's arm even through his winter coat. Just then, Chuck pulled out a Planter's Peanut brittle bar out of his pocket.

"Hey! I didn't see you buy that," said Jiff.

"'Cause I didn't," said Chuck.

"Huh?"

"Didn't buy it," Chuck affirmed.

"Then what're you doin' with it in your hand?"

"Helped myself to it," said Chuck nonchalantly.

"You stole it?" gasped Jiff, eyes wide.

"You wanna call it that," said Chuck, taking a bite into the bar. "My brother calls it a five finger discount."

Jiff laughed. "How did ya do it?"

"Nothin' to it. I was lookin' behind that last row of shelves where they store stuff and saw a whole case of peanut bars. No one was lookin' so I took one. They'll never miss it."

"I'm gonna try it," decided Jiff suddenly, turning back.

"You really gonna do it?" asked Guy, surprised.

"Sure!"

Jiff returned to the store and a few minutes later, came out again, walking casually as if nothing were amiss. But when he reached the street, he broke into a run and when he caught up to the others, pulled out a Planter's bar in triumph.

"You were right, Chuck," he said. "Super easy!"

"What did I tell ya?"

"You gonna try next, Guy?" asked Jiff, smiling.

"Not after two visits by you guys," said Guy. "They'll be suspicious for sure."

"He's right," said Chuck. "We gotta think these things out."

"Sounds like you wanna try again," noted Jiff, ripping into his stolen candy bar.

"I am. Wanna go down to Marie's and try it there?"

Jiff shrugged.

"Not today," said Guy. "I gotta get home for supper and then do my papers."

"Tomorrow then," said Jiff, eager to see how Guy would do.

"Sure," agreed Guy, not sure he liked the notion but couldn't help wanting to find out if he could get away with it.

The next day, they headed to Marie's this time in company with Mike and Don who'd been briefed on the previous day's triumphs. They too were eager to see how Guy would do.

"Okay, this is the plan," Chuck was saying. "We'll all go in and while the rest of us go to the end of the store where the register is, Guy'll make his move."

"What're ya gonna steal?" asked Mike, already eager for his turn.

Guy shrugged. "Dunno."

When they entered Marie's the others drifted to the farther end of the store, making as if they couldn't decide what soda pop flavor to buy at the big cooler across from the register. Guy held back, taking note of where Marie was in the store while at the same time, pretending to check out the various boxes of candy, pretzel rods, and notions that crowded the counter and helped to hide Marie from view. Suddenly nervous and fearful of the consequences of getting caught, Guy hesitated, making sure no other customers were around. While keeping his eye on the register area, he reached out and grabbed whatever his hand came into contact with and shoved it quickly out of sight into his pants pocket. He lingered in the area so as not to cast suspicion by leaving it suddenly. Slowly, he meandered in the direction of the others and eventually joined them in their discussion. When he did, they got the message and appeared to give up on the soda and headed for the door.

Outside, they walked in silence until they'd rounded the corner of the building then burst out with questions for Guy.

"Did you get something?" asked Mike.

"What'd you get?" asked Jiff.

Guy pulled out the object he'd secreted into his pocket: a pack of *Rat Patrol* trading cards.

"Cool!" said Don.

Guy himself was surprised and happy with his booty. He collected the *Rat Patrol* cards so this prize was doubly satisfying.

"I wanna try next," said Mike.

"Sure, sure," said Chuck, who was having a good time taking charge of the whole operation. "I got an idea. Why don't we let Mike and Don try their hand at it at different stores and if they get away with it like we did, I got a great idea for a real big job!"

"Whadaya have in mind?" asked Jiff.

"Not tellin' till we know if Mike and Don can handle it," he said.

"Hey! You puttin' us down?" demanded Don, always sensitive about the two year difference in their ages.

"Relax," soothed Chuck. "You know what I mean. We don't want any inexperienced yokels goin' with us and maybe spoilin' the works."

"Chuck's right," agreed Jiff. "You gotta start slow before tacklin' bigger game."

"Oh, okay," said Don, reconciled. "So when do we start?"

"I know a couple other variety stores we can go to," said Chuck. "We'll do it the same way we did it at Marie's. You game?"

Everyone agreed.

An hour later, the gang was walking slowly back to Desrosiers Street, their mouths filled with chewing gum Mike had stuffed his pockets with at Dell's Deli and Don was showing off the balsa wood airplane he'd slipped up the long sleeve of his shirt.

"Whadaya think?" he said. "Me and Mike are as good as you guys?"

The challenge was made with the confidence that the two had outdid the older boys with their stolen items.

"I never doubted you," said Guy.

"Me neither," agreed Jiff, almost choking on the huge wad of gum he was trying to chew.

"So what's this big score you had in mind, Chuck?" asked Don.

By then, they'd returned to the neighborhood and after trudging up through the crusty snow that still covered the Jorgenson's field, they climbed a tree that grew alongside the garage and clambered onto the roof. Sitting on the slope of the roof that faced away from the house and that looked over the still partially frozen swamp, they huddled around Chuck.

"Well?" persisted Mike.

"Take it easy," said Chuck, enjoying keeping the others in suspense.

"Okay, forget it then," said Mike dismissively.

"Spill it, Chuck," said Jiff.

"Okay, here it is," said Chuck, lowering his voice and seeming to bring the others into his confidence. "Just one word: The Bon Marche."

"That's three words," noted Don.

"Never mind that," said Jiff. "The big department store downtown?"

Chuck nodded. "Lots of people there to keep the clerks busy so they won't be paying much attention to kids like us. And they got a big toy department."

Jiff nodded his agreement. "Yeah!"

The others caught Jiff's enthusiasm and began to talk excitedly about what they'd do once they were in the store.

"When do we go?" asked Guy, caught up in the pending adventure.

Chuck shrugged. "What day do you think is the busiest?"

"Saturdays," said Guy, remembering the times when he was a kid and going on shopping trips downtown with his mother. "The store's crammed on Saturdays."

"Okay, we'll do it this Saturday," said Chuck.

Whenever the boys were together over the next few days, conversation inevitably came around to their pending expedition to the Bon Marche. How they'd operate, which departments they'd visit, what they intended to sneak away with. Soon, it became a challenge they gave each other to see who could walk away with the most interesting item.

Finally, the day arrived and the plan was to reach downtown by mid-morning. Guy needed to be back later in the afternoon to do his Saturday papers.

By the time they entered the downtown area, sidewalks were already bustling with shoppers and Merrimack Street leading from City Hall at one end to the Lowell Sun Building on the other, was busy with traffic. The cold, early spring day didn't seem to discourage anyone from getting out and about.

"Brrr!" said Jiff, shivering. "I should've worn a heavier coat."

"That's what you get for trying to push the season," said Guy, who always made sure to dress for the worst possible weather.

"Never mind about that," chided Chuck. "C'mon, let's stop over here a second and go over the plan."

"Aw, why do we need to do that?" complained Mike. "We know what we're gonna do."

"So no one makes any mistakes and knows what everyone else is gonna be doin' while they do their own thing," said Chuck.

They'd reached an alley formed by a church and the rear of the Bon Marche. There, Chuck took a seat on some stone steps leading into the church, unaware of the irony. The others remained standing.

"First, we go into the store one at a time so that we don't draw attention to ourselves," said Chuck. "If we go in all together, we're gonna attract the attention of the store detective."

"I never heard of such a thing," said Mike. "Stores have their own detectives?"

"Of course! They walk around like they're one of the customers but really they're keepin' an eye out for suspicious lookin' characters. A bunch o' kids like us comin' in all together is bound to grab his attention."

"But if he isn't wearin' a badge or somethin', how can we recognize 'em?"

"We don't. But we won't need to if we follow the plan."

Mike shrugged.

"Okay, then. We go in one at a time and head for whatever part of the store we want. Once we get what we want, just keep lookin' around a while before headin' to the door. We'll all meet here after to see who got the best stuff. Got it?"

The others nodded.

"Then let's go. I'll go in first."

Leading the way around from the church to Merrimack Street, Chuck mixed in with a line of people heading into the store.

One by one, the others did the same with Guy going last. In the excitement of the moment, he gave no thought to the right or wrong of what he intended to do. He saw it as a game, a fun challenge in competition with the others.

Passing through the revolving doors at the entrance to the store, Guy recognized the floor plan from his many visits there with his mother. On the left were the pair of elevators and stairs leading to the three upper floors and on the right, a maze of glass display cases belonging to the jewelry and perfume departments. Toward the back stood some mannequins showing off the latest styles in women's clothes. The floor space between them all was crowded with shoppers and clerks were busy at registers and demonstrating product.

Guy tried to spot the store detective but gave up. If there was one there, he was really good at making himself inconspicuous.

Intending to go to the toy department on the second floor, Guy headed to the elevators. There, he spotted Don and Mike waiting with a bunch of other people for a car to become available. Instead of joining them, he headed for the stairs and walked up instead.

Reaching the second floor, he paused slightly at the top of the stairs and looked around. Here, the floor wasn't as crowded as downstairs but there were still plenty of shoppers meandering about. Directly in front of him was the dinnerware department and beyond that, the bedding and kitchenware departments. But he knew where he was going and rounded the corner to the back side of the stairs where the toy department was.

It was a good deal more quiet here with mostly kids looking around while their mothers were busy checking out pillow cases and slip covers. Almost immediately, Guy spotted Chuck in one of the aisles. They made eye contact but otherwise avoided any overt display of recognition.

Guy went in the opposite direction and began looking around. He needed to find something he wanted but that could fit easily in his pocket or inside his coat. After a few minutes, he found a spinner rack filled with notions like super balls, silly putty, jacks, magic tricks, play money and such. He walked past it like he wasn't interested, finished making a circuit of the rest of the department (during which he lost track of Chuck but spotted Mike and Don coming in), then drifted back to the spinner.

While he looked around, he made sure to spot where any clerks or store employees were. At the last minute, he noticed a big convex mirror fixed to the wall up near the ceiling! His heart leaped into his throat as he contemplated the close call! What if he'd taken something in the range of that mirror? He might have been caught! Now, his hands shaking slightly, he approached the spinner, noting that from where it was, the mirrors were out of sight. And when the last browser was gone, he slipped a bag of plastic army tanks under his coat They could always use more military vehicles when he and Jiff played little army men.

Wasting little time now, he quickly left the department and, choosing the stairs again instead of a crowded elevator car, made it downstairs and out the door before the store detective, wherever he was, could stop him.

Outside, he breathed a heavy sigh of relief and ran as fast as he could around the corner to the meeting place. When he reached the alley, he found that he was the last to arrive.

"What'd ya get?" Mike wanted to know.

183

Guy pulled out the package of toy army tanks from beneath his coat.

"Cool!" said Mike.

Then the others displayed their own trophies: Don had grabbed a harmonica; Mike, a tube of model glue; Chuck, a package of Pez candies with a Popeye dispenser. But it was Jiff who amazed them all.

"Look what I got," he said, pulling out a pair of binoculars from his coat. And not just any old kids' binoculars, real professional ones!

"Wow!" said Don, echoing the gasps of amazement that came from everyone else.

"Lemme see those," demanded Chuck, taking them from Jiff and looking through the lenses. He fiddled with the adjustments for a few seconds. "These are incredible!"

While the binoculars were passed around, Jiff said: "I knew all you guys would head for the toy department so I decided to mosey over to sporting goods instead. There was hardly anyone there and no clerks either. So it was easy to snatch the binoculars."

"What about mirrors?" asked Don.

"Mirrors?"

"Yeah, they had them near the ceiling in the toy department so clerks could see around corners and over the shelves."

"Didn't notice any."

Don shook his head. "Boy, you were lucky you weren't spotted!"

Handing the binoculars back to Jiff, Guy was suddenly overcome by a feeling of anti-climax. He should've felt triumphant at their successful excursion. Instead, he felt like a heel. Why was that? Well, he knew the reason. It was the binoculars that did it. They weren't just cheap candy or plastic toys, they were a professional tool intended for adult use. They were real and expensive. What they were doing for a lark had serious consequences. In short, they were stealing. Someone paid for those binoculars, even if it was some rich owner of the Bon Marche. And they just stole the guy's property. It all just didn't sit right with Guy and stayed with him long after the gang had returned home.

Thoughtful and struggling with his conscience, Guy couldn't just go on with the others, he had to get away. And as usual when those moods struck him, that meant his tree platform. He was quiet during lunch at home, not participating in the banter between his siblings. He'd left the package of plastic tanks in his room, unopened. Then, aware that he had a few hours more before having to do his papers, he entered the woods at the end of the street and made his way through the still denuded trees and underbrush toward Beaver Brook. Overhead, the sky had clouded over bringing the temperatures down. Somehow, the gray, cheerless day matched his mood. Zipping his coat up to the collar, he broke through the final barrier to the old maple tree and began climbing the wooden rungs nailed into the rough bark.

Passing through the opening in the platform, he threw himself down to think.

Why did I do that? he asked himself for the hundredth time. *Why did I go ahead and steal that stuff? Why do I listen to Chuck at all?*

It was a question that he'd been wrestling with for some time without realizing it.

It had become so typical for Chuck to suggest something and everyone else would just agree and follow him. And just as typically, Guy would feel guilty afterward when it was too late to do anything about it. How did Chuck get them all to go along with what he wanted? Whether it was spitting or drinking and smoking, or now shoplifting. Was he that persuasive or was it the lure of the forbidden that drew them on? Or was it something deeper? Was it what he learned about in religion class; just human nature born of original sin? *Nah,* Guy thought, *too simple.* What it was was that none of them took the time to think things through before they did them. They didn't consider the consequences or the harm they did, only the fun.

The more he thought about it, the more he was convinced that Chuck was at the root of whatever it was that was eating at the relationship between himself and his friends. *Things had been so simple before Chuck came along,* he thought. Now, even Jiff was slowly drifting away from him. He no longer read comics and had even cut way back on his reading; both interests they used to share but now barely ever even mentioned to each other. Suddenly, a new realization occurred to Guy: he was losing his best friend and the person who was driving a wedge between them was Chuck!

CHAPTER TWELVE

In which Guy receives a sign from God

It happened out of the blue.

Or was it out of the blue? Didn't the same thing happen once before when he graduated from the academy and was instantly assigned as executive officer of the *Attacker?*

Or maybe Someone Up There was keeping an eye out for him?

Nick was very much inclined to believe it. How else to explain his being called into Staff upon completion of the *Attacker's* mission to the asteroid belt and being told that he would have command of a brand new ship called the *Marauder?*

Nick could hardly believe it and since he could pick his own crew, the first person he chose to be his second was good old Dan.

"All right!" said Dan upon hearing the news. "Now we'll show this Force how a tight ship is run!"

"You said it," agreed a grinning Nick.

"It's just too bad Buster couldn't have been with us," said Dan. "But after the stuff he did, you were right in having him drummed out of the Force."

Nick had not liked doing that, but it was something that had to be done. And who knew? Maybe it had to be done in order for this new windfall to happen. Fate certainly worked in mysterious ways.

Gateway to the Future
Guy DeMonde

It was later in the spring with only a few more weeks before school let out for the summer, but unlike past years, the excitement of being free from homework and classes didn't grab Guy as much as it used to. Concerns over Chuck's negative influence and his weakening ties with Jiff conspired to keep him from feeling completely happy. That, and the end of his relationship with Michelle LaRochelle. Not that there ever really was one, but it had been nice to imagine that there *could* have been.

It happened this way.

"Deni Cardolet, Paul Bouchon, Lise O'Kelly, Guy DeMonde, and Michelle LaRochelle," said Soeur Yvette, reading from a prepared list.

Guy was in science class that day, mostly daydreaming, when Soeur Yvette informed the class that they were to break down into separate study groups with each to cover different aspects of biology.

Normally, when the class broke down into groups, part of the new style of teaching that some teachers were eager to indulge in, Guy only paid attention to see if he'd be paired with one of his friends. But when Michelle's name was mentioned in the same breath as his own, he perked up.

I'm going to be in a group with Michelle? he asked himself wonderingly.

Was he dreaming?

But it was true!

Great!

Even as he looked, his fellow students rose from their places and began sorting themselves out according to the groups Soeur Yvette had outlined. Eagerly, he looked for Michelle and spotted her getting up from where she sat at the head of the class. As if in a dream, he found himself following her as she joined Deni and Lise and the others.

"Deni," called out Soeur Yvette. "You'll take your group into the lab."

"*Oui, ma Soeur,*" said Deni, obediently.

Guy couldn't help feeling resentment toward Deni. Not only was he the most popular kid in class and the fastest runner, but he was a straight A student and a darling of the faculty. Not only that, but as an altar boy, he also managed to snag all the funeral Masses too. Now, Soeur Yvette was making him the defacto leader of the study group.

But just then, Guy didn't care. He was happy that he was in that same group with Michelle. Frightened that she might guess he was sweet on her, Guy tried to act casual but couldn't help admiring her whenever he could. He didn't know what the tastes of the other boys in the class were, but to him, Michelle was easily the most attractive among the girls. Seeing her now close up, he couldn't help wondering how different she appeared in her school uniform with pleated jumper and white blouse compared to the "civilian" garb he'd seen her wear at St. Louis Park. He couldn't decide which he preferred.

He'd been so busy thinking about Michelle that he never noticed that the group had moved into the gloomy lab room that was adjacent to their regular classroom. Another group had followed them in and gathered at a lab bench on the other side of the room along the back windows that overlooked the schoolyard.

"Okay, guess the first thing we oughtta do is decide which parts of the project each of us will take on," said Deni. He was standing at a second lab bench nearer the door that connected to the classroom on the other side.

"I'll take ants as the study subject," said Paul.

"I'm not particularly crazy about bugs," admitted Lise. "But I'll take their physical structure."

"Swell! Hey, I think we're making good progress already," enthused Deni. "What about you, Michelle?"

"I'm not interested in this whole damn class," laughed Michelle and everyone else joined her.

Everyone except Guy.

He was stunned!

Never had he expected that kind of language from Michelle! In his mind, she'd been flawless, the idealization of all female kind; the sweet, charming girl who would understand him the way no one else did. In his mind, he'd imagined her to be the perfect confidant, the one who'd never disappoint him. And now, she had! As he'd done with the spitting habit, Guy had trained himself not to use foul language under any circumstances because it was the kind of language he associated with the punk kids he hated. Never, in his life would he have dreamed Michelle would indulge in the same bad habit!

It was as if a veil had been ripped away to reveal ugliness underneath or a rock tipped over to expose a big, slimy worm.

Suddenly, in a single moment, all of his tender feelings for Michelle vanished. The revelation had left him cold and bitterly disappointed.

What do I do now? he asked himself. He hadn't realized how much he'd built up Michelle in his own mind. How important she'd become to his morale.

"Hey, Guy, wake up," someone was saying.

"I think he's daydreaming again," said someone else. And Guy realized it was Michelle.

But where only a few moments before, he would've been thrilled to hear her address him in any kind of way, now it meant nothing. Nothing at all.

"Oh, I guess I'll do the introduction," said Guy at last. "The rest of you will either have to give me a summary of your parts of the project, or I'll have to wait until your all done before I can start writing it."

"Good enough," said Deni. "But I think it'll be better if we give Guy the summaries so he doesn't get rushed at the end. We don't want to miss the deadline. You all know how Soeur Yvette can be."

They all laughed and joked some at the sister's expense.

But Guy remained mostly silent. Too disenchanted at having all his pleasant dreams of Michelle shattered. It had all been an illusion. A foundation built on sand, the kind of shifting sands he and Jiff used to play little army men in…

"Hey, Guy! If you don't keep your mind on what your doin' you're gonna lose out."

"Huh? Oh, yeah. Keep throwin'."

"Here comes a tank," said Jiff from where he sat perched on the railing surrounding his front porch.

Jiff had decided that he was no longer interested in playing little army men and when both Guy and Don expressed interest in his army set, he decided to hold a contest of sorts that involved his throwing one piece at a time from the porch down into the backyard where Guy and Don would be forced to scramble to recover the thrown piece before the other could grab it.

Guy stared at the small pile of plastic army men and assorted accessories that he'd managed to recover but his success wasn't as satisfying as he'd thought. No sooner had he run to fetch the first piece thrown than he felt an overwhelming sense of humiliation. What was he doing down here while Jiff sat up there lording it over him and watching him scramble for any piece he threw? The more he considered it, the redder he felt his face becoming.

Going out to his tree platform to be by himself and think always cleared his mind and helped him make better sense of things. His new determination that Chuck's interests weren't for him, that in fact, they ran against everything Guy felt himself to be, and what he wanted to be was good, not bad. He'd given up spitting and vowed to himself never to indulge in foul language, and luckily the problem of wine coolers and tiparellos and rambling was solved for him with time and the passage of winter. As a result, his mind had grown clearer and his conscience freed. He felt sure that he'd begun on a road that was more his own than one chosen by Chuck. He'd make his own path and not be a follower.

But then, where did that leave him and Jiff? Did he break away from Chuck only to end up being a follower for Jiff? He remembered how he tried to dress like Jiff and more recently, copying trends that Jiff had adopted from his classmates at school, he and the others had taken to wearing their shirts untucked with the tails hanging out, and disdaining wearing white socks. And now, here he was waiting on Jiff as he tossed bits of his army set and watched as Guy and Don scampered to get the best pieces.

Already depressed over the loss of Michelle, Guy was no longer in the mood for this.

"Hey, Guy! Where you goin'?" called Jiff, as Guy turned to go.

"You can have it all, Don," said Guy in a voice lacking emotion. "I'm not interested."

"Why not? What happened?"

"I dunno," said Guy, pausing. "I just...I dunno."

Guy started walking across the front yard, headed for home. Suddenly he felt like losing himself in his comic book collection, the only sure fire thing that could lift him out of the dumps.

"I'll see ya later, Jiff," he said in parting.

"Okay, Guy," said Jiff, shrugging for Don's benefit.

"I'll be up there in a minute," said Don, collecting what pieces he'd picked up as well as those left behind by Guy. "The whole set's mine now!"

The next day, Guy remained somewhat flustered and out of sorts. For the first time in known memory, he didn't feel like going over to the Jorgenson's house and calling for Jiff in the old sing song way they always used.

Instead, he grabbed the book he was reading and headed out to the tree platform.

It was about mid spring with the temperatures finally warming up. There was bright sunshine overhead and so warm that morning that only a sweatshirt was needed to keep the chill out. It was a combination that Guy had learned to love: a good sweatshirt and being out in the woods by himself, alone with his thoughts. More than once, he'd broken a writer's block out here when the literary problem he wrestled with seemed insoluble anywhere else.

Reaching the tree, he clambered up to the platform and sat down, looking up between the branches into a featureless blue sky broken only by branches that so far sported only the red buds that came before the green leafage that would soon obscure his view.

From up here, he could catch glimpses of the Merrimack glistening in the morning sunlight, and houses that comprised the Centralville neighborhoods and the top floor of St. Louis School poking up among them. Next to it was the bell tower of the modernesque St. Louis Church and farther away, the tall smokestacks of the city's old mill buildings. Next, in the near distance was Lookout Hill and beyond it, the Old House that marked the edge of town.

Sighing loudly, he opened his book and began to read about the valor and faith of the Knights Hospitaller and their epic battles defending Christianity against the hordes of Islam first in the Holy Land, then on the island of Rhodes, and finally on Malta. Throughout, their dogged example inspired Guy in his own faith, encouraging him, in some small way, to live up to the Knights' standards. For him, that meant a growing determination not to fall into the habits of others simply in an effort to get along by going along. More and more, he wanted to be his own self, carving and sculpting his own personality out of a desire to be good and not bad like the punk kids he detested. Striving to be good was his way of defying those kinds of negative qualities, of being independent, and not being led, not by Chuck nor even by Jiff. He had his own interests to sustain him: his comics, his reading, his interest in science fiction and history, his writing, his family, and his confidence that he could make it alone if he had to even if the price was giving up on girls like Michelle if they disappointed him.

It occurred to him then that he'd always known the right path to take but for the most part, ignored the voice inside him that tried to give warning when something he was doing didn't fit with the values he'd been taught.

Newly inspired and determined, Guy left the tree platform and made his way back through the brush, the stand of pine forest, and up the grassy slope of Lookout Hill. At the top, he paused to breathe in the fresh air with its scents of spring and to survey the world around him, out to the horizon and beyond. He was certain now that he'd placed himself on the right track. He saw the way laid out ahead of him and it would be easy to follow if he had the will. Just then, the bells from St. Louis Church began to peal in the distance, as if putting the finishing touch on his ruminations. Was it coincidence? Or was God signaling approval of his effort to reinvent himself?

Guy was still wondering about it as he retraced his steps toward home when he was met by Trece and Marie who seemed filled with excitement.

"What's the matter?" asked Guy as he jumped down from the old wooden fence that blocked the end of the street.

"You won't believe it," gasped Marie.

"What? What is it?"

"The moving van is already there!"

"Moving van? What moving van?"

"Over there," said Trece, pointing next door.

Guy could see the big, red and white truck indicated by his sister, but his mind refused to draw the proper conclusion.

"Can't you see?" asked Trece, frustrated at his consternation. "Chuck is moving!"

CHAPTER THIRTEEN

*In which Guy experiences an ending
and a new beginning*

Nick Tropoli stood on the bridge of the newly commissioned *Marauder*.

Beside him stood his executive officer and good friend, Dan Montez.

"Where are we bound to Captain?" asked Dan, smiling.

"Phobos," replied Nick. "One of Mars' two moons. Seems we have some civilians to pick up."

"Must be bigwigs to rate the *Marauder* for simple taxi service."

"Just a group of scientists and their support staff on routine rotation."

"Well, if you'll forgive me, sir," said Dan with a wink. "I hope we find some adventure there anyway."

Nick said nothing but could not help a feeling that something or someone on Phobos would end up disrupting his so far charmed life. Everything was going so smoothly. What could possibly go wrong?

Gateway to the Future
Guy DeMonde

Guy always wondered if it had been a miracle.

First, straightening out his thoughts and feelings at the tree platform, then hearing the sound of the bells from St. Louis as if God was trying to tell him he was on the right track, and then the electrifying news that Chuck's family was moving out of the neighborhood and possibly out of his life!

"How come you didn't tell us?" asked Jiff, later that day.

He, Guy, Mike, Don, and Chuck were gathered at the top of Desrosiers Street where it intersected with Dean, watching as the movers carried out the Lavalle's belongings and storing them in the big moving van.

Chuck shrugged helplessly. "I didn't know myself until the last minute. The van was already out front when my Dad told me."

"C'mon!" said Don, in disbelief.

"Well, almost," insisted Chuck.

"Where are ya movin' to?" asked Guy. He didn't say so, but hoped it was far enough to make continued association with Chuck unlikely.

"In Lowell somewhere," replied Chuck. "On the other side of town."

"Wow," said Mike, sounding disappointed.

"It's gonna be pretty dull around here without ya," said Jiff.

"Yeah," laughed Chuck. "You guys are such old sticks in the mud!"

"We'll get by," said Don.

Chuck took out his pocket knife and flipped open the blade. He threw it at the ground by the side of the road where it stuck in deep. Leaning over, he spit across the knife.

"For luck," he said, stooping over to pluck the knife from the ground.

Guy said nothing, convinced that he'd been right in his assessment of Chuck. He *was* a bad influence.

"Your father's calling you," said Mike, inclining his chin in the direction of the movers.

"Yeah, he wants me to help bring some stuff to the car," observed Chuck. "Guess this is it. See ya around."

"See ya," said the others in a ragged chorus. Mike giving a small wave.

They remained to watch Chuck and his brother finish helping their father load the station wagon. Then, the movers closed up the truck while Mr. Lavalle locked the door to the apartment.

With a rev of its engine, the big moving van pulled out of the driveway followed by the station wagon. As the little caravan made the bend over to Dean Avenue and down to Lakeview, the gang waved again in goodbye. A hand waved back from an open window and then Chuck was gone leaving everyone with an empty feeling.

Everyone, that is, except Guy.

To Guy, Chuck's leaving was a relief.

He'd felt for a long time that something hadn't been quite right between he and his friends. Unable to speak for the others, Guy realized now that he'd only been fooling himself when he made excuses for the things he did with Chuck. He'd known all the time that they were wrong. But now, with Chuck gone, there was a chance for them to return to an earlier, cleaner, golden age before the spitting and the rambling and the shoplifting.

Thinking further on the meaning of the moment, Guy found himself glad that he'd sorted out his feelings earlier, before he found out that Chuck was moving. If he hadn't, how would he have known if he'd arrived at his decision because it was what he wanted to do or simply because he had no choice? The way things turned out, he'd *had* a choice and made it on his own without being forced.

He knew now that he had the strength of character to change his life if he wanted to; he didn't have to follow anyone else. He could be something new and unique. He could invent himself!

No sooner did Chuck move out than what Guy had hoped would happen, happened. Namely, a return of the cozy relationship among his friends and especially between he and Jiff. Once again, they were best friends, calling on each other in the familiar sing song manner, exploring the nearby woods, and even playing army as the Monkey Division with Mike and Don.

And to Guy's infinite joy, Jiff's interest in comics had been rekindled somewhat with Guy quickly bringing him up to speed on the doings of the Fantastic Four, Spider-Man, and Thor. They began to trade science fiction books back and forth and enthusiastically discussing the pros and cons of Ray Bradbury, Isaac Asimov, and Philip K. Dick. Why, even Mike started getting into science fiction!

It seemed to be a new golden age and all was right with the world as Guy sailed through those warming summer days filled with running, and bike riding, and dreaming. He didn't know it at the time, but that summer marked his last vacation in Salem, and he spent more time alone up in his tree platform, marveling at how wonderful things had turned out after Chuck left. Somewhere in his mind, he felt sorry for his former friend. He could only imagine that with his family situation and his brother's negative influence, that Chuck would not have the grounding needed to break free. In those moments, Guy thanked God for his own family and friends who supplied him with the kind of support that Chuck was denied.

Yeah, life is good, thought a contented Guy, as he leaned back against the tree, hands behind his head, and stared up from the green leaves overhead to the featureless blue sky beyond.

The only thing he could think of that could possible upset things now was the sale of the Ohlenbeck's house.

Because as it turned out, Chuck's family weren't the only ones to move out of the neighborhood that summer of 1967. Directly across the street from Guy, the Ohlenbeck's also departed, leaving their pretty cottage up for sale. Whether that boded good or ill, only time would tell.

"I saw the big moving van in front of the Ohlenbeck's yesterday," Jiff was saying.

He, Don, Mike, and Guy were hanging around the swings in the DeMonde's back yard. Across the street, the Ohlenbeck's house was quiet, but for how long?

"Yeah, I guess they're done movin' in now," said Guy.

"I didn't see any kids around," noted Mike.

"What about it, Guy? Any kids?" prompted Jiff. But Guy knew he meant any boys.

Guy shook his head. "Didn't see any kids. Only the father. Or at least I think it was the father."

"Got bad news for ya," said Don. "I heard my mother talkin' to Mrs. Beaudoin who lives next door, and they said somethin' about a girl."

There was a collective groan among the boys, but Guy had mixed feelings. Recalling their experience with Chuck, he was relieved that there wouldn't be another chance of having to go through something like that again. But on the other hand, it would've been nice to have another guy in the neighborhood so long as he fit in.

"Just what we need, another girl," said Mike.

Both Jiff and Guy were silent. They'd arrived at the point where girls weren't to be considered the nuisance they'd always seemed before...unless they were your sisters.

It was a week later that Guy had the chance to reassess that evaluation.

He was in the Dracut Library checking to see if they had any more Tarzan books he hadn't read before when he was approached by Polly Cardona in company with another girl he didn't recognize.

"I should've known you'd be here," said Polly.

Guy rose to his feet from where he'd been crouching to get a better look at the lower shelves. The new girl had blond hair, like Michelle.

"This is Noel," said Polly. "She's the new girl who moved in across the street from you."

She's kinda cute, admitted Guy to himself, but immediately suppressed the thought. *No way am I going to get burned again.*

But whether he'd regret it or not, remained to be seen because that, as they say, was a story for another day!

EPILOGUE

Over the course of three crucial years, years filled with key events and turning points (most of which had gone unrecognized), Guy had molded himself into a different kind of person than he was before. The foundation of which was an instinct to shy away from anything that smacked of conformity, of being too much like other people.

He was attracted to organizations like the military and the Boy Scouts and even the priesthood but knew he'd find it impossible to conform to their rules and follow orders.

Although not yet firm, he'd begun a process of re-invention that left him different from other youngsters his age. Something he sensed early on in his solitary walks, his active imagination, and instances where he often preferred to be by himself than with others.

His interests in science fiction made him a member of a very small club (when his friends lost interest, he soldiered on by himself). And his continued interest in comic books to an even smaller one. His pursuit of writing was an intensely personal endeavor misunderstood by everyone he knew. His successes and failures (mostly failures) were suffered alone with no one interested in reading what he'd written.

His penchant for taking long sojourns in the woods by himself confirmed his solitary nature. Like the androids and mutants he'd read about in science fiction novels, he was a new kind of person, different from anyone else his own age. (Or so it seemed to him at the time) He seemed able to stand outside the hurly burly of life and look at the rest of the world objectively without emotion getting in the way. The better to pick and choose the elements he needed to make up his character. The person *he* wanted to be and not whom others wanted him to be. He was, finally, his own man.

All easy enough to say until Guy was faced with the greatest challenge to his sense of himself. One that had already moved in across the street from him...